The Road from La Cueva

The Road
from
La Cueva

A Novel
by
Sheila Ortego

Dianne,
Thank you for your
support!
love,
Sheila

SUNSTONE
PRESS

SANTA FE

Book and cover design by Vicki Ahl

Sunstone books may be purchased for educational, business, or sales promotional
use. For information please write: Special Markets Department, Sunstone Press,
P.O. Box 2321, Santa Fe, New Mexico 87504-2321.

Library of Congress Cataloging-in-Publication Data

Ortego, Sheila, 1952-
    The road from La Cueva : a novel / by Sheila Ortego.
        p. cm.
    ISBN 978-0-86534-588-1 (alk. paper)
    I. Title.

PS3615.R73R63 2007
863'.7--dc22

                                        2007040381

WWW.SUNSTONEPRESS.COM
SUNSTONE PRESS / POST OFFICE BOX 2321 / SANTA FE, NM 87504-2321 /USA
(505) 988-4418 / ORDERS ONLY (800) 243-5644 / FAX (505) 988-1025

For Louis Ortego-
I see you still, your lantern
swinging, your golden light
on mossy water.

1

*A*na's shift at St. Joseph's had ended. The road ahead was a familiar ordeal. At La Cueva, thirty miles from town, the battered cattle gate came into view, chained and padlocked on its cedar post. A late November snow had come, turning the road to muck. She had to get out to open the gate, slogging ankle-deep in *caliche*, then back to the Wagoneer to drive through, and out again, to shut it. It would be a hard drive to get through the ditches carved in the road and up the slippery hills. The last stretch was a bog full of boulders, curved and slick as turtlebacks. She was grateful her daughter Emmy was at home with Frank. If not for that, there would have been the worry of sending the Wagon into a slide, of crushing it to a coffin of twisted steel.

She gunned the engine. Mud ground into wheel wells and sloshed across the Wagon's rusted-out fenders. She had to floor it to get past Henry's concrete-block house, plowing new troughs into the clay. When it dried, the road looked like a seismic disaster. Even when the road wasn't bad, there was always the problem of getting past Henry and his rottweilers. This time the self-named guardian of the gate at the bottom of the road wasn't home. His faded green Chevy wasn't in the driveway, which was good, since the Wagon careened across a corner of it, turning his well-graveled path to a churned, soggy hole. Ana squinted, searching the forest for the dogs. They hid themselves well in the dense juniper, piñon, and cedar, but she knew, at any moment, they could bolt. And they did. She heard them barking, then saw them, shadow-forms racing after her, snarling as she passed. She shoved on, losing them at the first bend. If she could make it up the hill, she'd have a good run at the waterlogged pit below, where a culvert should have been.

But there was to be no good run. The Wagon strained to get to the top of the hill. Below, crawling out of the pit, was a mud-spattered Volkswagen Bug. Kay Scudder, Ana's closest neighbor, gripped the steering wheel, straining her skinny chest against it. The Bug lurched toward the Wagon in slow motion, balding tires grinding helplessly in the mire. Neither could stop, or they'd be stuck. Or one might fishtail into the other, or slide off the shoulder and into the ditch. The Wagon's headlights lit Kay's face dimly behind a mud-splashed windshield, a pale blur framed in its cap of limp, yellow hair. Ana jerked the wheel to the right, shoved her foot hard against the pedal, and managed to pull clear.

Kay's husband Dean came into view at the next bend, slouching on the porch of their rotting A-Frame. Ana could just make out the shape of his arm in the darkness, curving to shelter a flicker of match flame as he lit a joint. Dean. Scudder. Like a bottom-feeding fish. Sometimes Kay's bright yellow hair was combed forward, hiding brown and purple bruises just the size and shape of his fist.

Ana didn't know what she'd done to deserve neighbors like this. It probably had something to do with the bargain price of the land they'd all bought. The only one she trusted was Margaret who lived farther up. Margaret didn't have a house–just a motor home that shined like a bright nickel from behind the trees, a home shared with dogs, cats, chickens, a blue parakeet. She had no electricity, and at first Ana didn't know how she lived without it. But later, she'd seen her carrying the green Coleman lanterns, had seen the makeshift stovepipe that pumped smoke out at sunrise and all day long in winter. The propane truck came to fill her tank every month or so, to run the little stove in the kitchenette. She did all right.

There was the water problem, though. Most of them had no wells and had to haul water in from Santa Fe. At least she and Frank had gotten a well with the land when they'd bought it. The developers said that doubled the price, but even with that, and despite the shape the road was in, it had seemed a good deal at the time. Five-acre lots facing east, mountains, plenty of good, raw nature. She believed she could make it into a home, something of her own.

Ana had followed Frank there only a few years ago, climbing after him when he walked over boulders big as elephants, standing behind him as he looked out over the ridge. Plum-colored mountains, snow on the trees, light clear as water. She had thought she'd never seen anything so beautiful, so perfect. She'd had faith, then. There was only a minute when she'd hesitated, when Frank said it was time to decide.

"What will we do for a house?" she'd asked.

"I'll build it," he said. "And I'll fix the road up. We can blade it out, put some gravel on it."

"But it's in such bad shape," she'd said. She had hated to argue with him. He seemed so confident.

"Sure, now it does," he said. "But just wait. I'll build a big house, and the road will be easy. I'll get a backhoe, put in some culverts. You'll see."

That had been six years ago, and still the road was a sinkhole, no culverts, no gravel. There was a house, though it was unfinished. Some of the windows were still boarded over, and there was bare sheetrock on the walls, floors missing tile. Frank had laid the foundation himself, working his strong, wiry arms, mixing cement in a battered wheelbarrow until his hands bled. He built it on the rock that forced its way through the land like the stubborn roots of a Chinese elm. The whole forest could have collapsed in a mudslide, but that house would still be there, Frank's blood holding it in place.

She pushed the Wagon past the Scudder's, through the worst of the pit. It did a long, slow fishtail, then lumbered up and out of the mire, hauling itself over a stretch of bare rock and onto the short, graveled driveway that led to home.

The living room was warm, the woodstove blazing with a neighbor's juniper. Frank didn't believe in cutting trees on his own land. He used a poker to jab at the burning logs, glancing at Ana as she opened the door, his jaw set in a stiff, hard line. There were the chiseled lips, almost hidden by a thick mustache, the sharp blue eyes, brows arching upward. His face had so appealed to her when they first met.

"I'm hungry," he said, before she had time to put down her purse.

A sigh rose inside her, but she swallowed it, pushing it back where it came from. "I'll make something," she said. She pulled off tennis shoes and rubbed the soles together, clearing the mud. It gathered and fell, clotted, onto a worn floor mat. She looked at Emmy, who sat on the piano bench, feeding a sock monkey from an empty spoon.

"What's Dooby eating?"

"Oatmeal," Emmy said. She held the spoon to Ana's lips. "Want some?"

"Not right now," Ana said. She opened the refrigerator. There was a bloody slab of elk venison, a bowl of day-old tuna salad. The sight of the elk made her gag, so she reached for the tuna.

"How's this?" She held the bowl out to Frank, an offering.

"All right." He put the poker away, lit a cigar, and slumped into his La-Z-Boy. When Ana handed him the plate, he picked at it with his fork.

"It has onions?"

"Sorry." She went back to the kitchen, started again. She found a can of tuna, mixed it with mayonnaise, and slapped it on the plate with a rebellious twist of the fork. But when she carried it back to him, she put it quietly on a small, round table, next to his ashtray.

There was no "thank you." Just the clink of his fork against the plate. Emmy reached up, latched her hands around Ana's waist, and climbed, curling in her arms. "Rock me," she said. She was almost five years old, but she still liked to be rocked to sleep, and Ana didn't mind. She took her to the bedroom, escaping the steady sound of Frank's chewing. She didn't know why it irritated her so much, made her want to scream.

Emmy settled into her lap in the rocking chair, and Ana read to her by the light of a brass table lamp with a dusty shade. The book was *Harold and the Purple Crayon*, the one she'd read to her a hundred times before. She studied Emmy, her freckled nose, round blue eyes, the white-blond hair in loose, unraveled braids, a patch of it hopelessly matted at the back of her head. She was beautiful in the same way Frank had been as a child, people said. Her eyes, especially, were his. Emmy seemed to belong to Frank, just as Ana had been her own father's daughter. Still, the child was Ana's anchor. She loved to hold her, the solid weight of her as she pushed the rocking chair forward and back. Emmy was going to sleep, her head tilting back, farther and farther. She had always been easy to carry, but lately this had begun to change. Ana leaned forward and pushed out of the chair. Her back strained as she stooped to put her in bed. This was still the same slight, almost delicate child, yet heavy, almost too heavy to hold. She tucked a quilt around Emmy's chin and stood up straight, stretched her back. Things wouldn't seem so hard tomorrow, when she wasn't so tired.

She looked to the new glass in the window, already smudged to gray by wind and rain. But she could still see through it-to trees that looked soft from a distance, to blue moonlight on drifted snow. Underneath the snow, she knew, there was mud, crushed beer cans, rusted rebar. But for now, the land was white, clean, like bleached bone.

◊ ◊ ◊

The evening shift Ana worked at St. Joseph's turned into a "full moon night," as the nurses called it. A grandfather sobbed in the waiting room, while the mother told the story. He had backed his truck out of the garage, running over his two-year-old grandson, killing him. A Mexican woman had stabbed her *gringo* husband. He'd called her a bitch, again. One time too many. A baby was born too soon, the tiny hands pale, limp. The mother bleeding on the gurney, red stain spreading on the sheets, the doctors hovering. Ana observed it only distantly, rushing through her rounds, drawing blood in the emergency room, the cardiac unit, intensive care, the psych ward, gathering blood in fat glass tubes, for the tests. Complete blood counts, chemistry surveys, drug screens. This was her skill, the one the techs had taught her on quiet nights at the lab. Frank had said he didn't want her to work-that he made plenty of money, she didn't need to. She'd won that battle, at least. He said she could work for a while, until the house was finished and the road was fixed.

When she started the job, she couldn't detach herself from what she saw: bodies, mangled and broken, the pale, sick flesh offered up to her needle. She took comfort in the company of the techs and nurses; they dragged her to Tino's after shifts had ended, made her watch while they numbed themselves with pitchers of beer. They tried to get her to drink, but she wouldn't. It was bad enough that she had to worry about what Frank would say if he knew where she was. They nagged her to play the tinny old piano at the back of the bar. There was a book of love songs inside the bench-a big book with a fat cover, drawings of ladies in long dresses, men in top-hats, faded valentines. *Silver Threads Among the Gold, Red River Valley, Auld Lang Syne.* The songs reminded Ana of her mother's old radio programs, songs full of love and regret, hopeless. Still, she gave in to them. She secretly craved the attention, the feeling that they admired her ability to play.

Tonight, when they asked if she'd meet them, she said she had to think about it. Frank would be mad if she was late again. The last time she came home past midnight, he warned her. All he said was, "You know better..." The way he said that, the most terrible thoughts came to her. She never knew what he was threatening, but she was sure he would follow through on whatever it was. Sometimes she didn't care. He could do what he wanted. But other times, like tonight, she didn't want to hear his questions, his veiled accusations. Besides, another soft, wet snow was beginning to fall. The road would swallow her along with the Wagon if she took too long to get home. So when they asked, she begged off, promising to go another time. She knew she would come home from work to find Frank sleeping in his La-Z-Boy, waiting for her. One of his arms would be cradling Emmy tenderly against his wiry chest, and she would be curled against him, like a kitten.

Ana's last patient was on the psych ward, a fifteen-year-old. He had sprayed gold paint into a paper bag and inhaled the fumes. His mouth and hands glittered like the paper art of a child, and his breath escaped in a haze of acetone. A filthy T-shirt hung from long, thin arms, and the eyes were open, unseeing, a flat, muddy color.

A man was writing notes in a chart. A man-a nurse, Ana realized. She cleared her throat to announce her presence, and he glanced at her.

"I'm here to get the blood tests," she said.

"Come in," he said, pulling the pale green curtain aside, starting to leave the room. Then he stopped, studying her. "Need help?" he asked. He didn't seem to mind the way Ana's eyebrows had lifted when she saw him. He probably knew by now how people reacted when they saw what he did: women's work. She studied him too, his tall, lanky body, his face a terrain of well-healed acne scars. The look was battle-worn, but not unattractive. His eyes were hazel, flecked with gold, and a shock of long chestnut hair was pulled back in a strip of red braided cloth. He moved to yield the narrow strip of linoleum beside the bed to her, but stood waiting, looking at her intently.

"Thanks, I can handle it," Ana said. She fumbled for her equipment, glancing up at him when she felt he had finally turned his eyes from her.

"I'll stay for a minute," he said. "In case you need me." He moved back in, close to her. He clamped a hand around the boy's wrist. There was no resistance.

"I'm Michael Woods," he said. "Just started the evening shift."

"Ana Howland," she said, puncturing a vein in the boy's arm, drawing thick, dark blood into a white syringe. She thought this Michael was feigning a casualness he did not truly feel. There was something in his eyes–searching. But she quickly shook off the feeling. It was silly. He had hardly said a thing. He was just being friendly, helpful, as anyone would be.

She tried to focus on the procedure, on how she handled the syringe, pulled the needle out, capped it, labeled tubes.

"You get many orders up here?" Michael cleared his throat. As if he wished he'd said something else. "On the psych ward, I mean."

"I go all over," she said. "Wherever they send me." She gathered up her tray, turned to leave the room.

"I'll look for you," he said. His hand reached for hers. It was warm, chapped, and it held her hand tightly, for a long time. The grip made her hold her breath, return his gaze. It was a look that let her know he meant what he said. He would look for her, he wanted to see her again. She pulled her hand away, suddenly shy. He smiled, gently, raised his hand in a wave goodbye, and left the curtain flapping behind him.

She turned her attention back to the boy. There were too many of these kids, defeated, hopeless. She'd been like that. Young, crazy. But she always thought the rest of the world was normal, that she was the only one who gave up, who didn't fight for something better. It seemed that way, growing up in her mother's church. That world was clean, milky-white, flawless. She never felt good enough to live in it. And then Frank had come along, and she had the idea he could save her from it, or from herself.

From the time he walked into the blood bank where she worked, she had thought Frank was different, special. He was handsome, in a rugged sort of way. She liked that. And he was bold. He knew what he was looking for. In the beginning she thought she understood him. He'd gone to college for one year, and then announced to his parents that every moment there had been useless and boring. Like her, he was an only child. His mother had a college degree, but he identified with his father, who didn't. Both Frank and his father believed uneducated women made better wives. His mother proved it by running off with a rich lawyer when he was in his teens. He forgave Ana for having a degree, since she already had it. As for his own education, he had gotten it on his own terms, from borrowed textbooks, from businessmen in bars. He'd worked odd jobs, building cabinets for a local contractor, welding, walking patrol as a security guard. He was working for a telephone company when Ana met him, and he liked to talk about how he'd taught himself to wiretap, how if he wanted to find something out, he could.

The plans he had for his life sounded real. He made Ana believe he was brilliant-a real man, like her father could have been, if not for her mother. The Frank she'd met seemed strong as hell, stubborn enough to do what he believed in, smart enough to know how to make it happen. Still, she had begun to wonder why she'd given so much of herself up for him. Her only excuse was that she hadn't seen it coming. She hadn't known she was about to lose the Ana Godreau yet to be discovered. She hadn't known she'd end up as Mrs. Frank Howland, a person she had never intended to be.

Despite all that, he asked little in return for what he offered. Only that she live by three simple rules: family first, no friends (other men), and to follow any new rules he came up with. It seemed a small price to pay. He said he loved her, and she knew the moment he said it, this was something she desperately wanted. Lately, it seemed he was always watching her, to see if she obeyed. She hadn't known, when she married him, how long the list of rules would be.

She remembered their wedding, the off-white dress sewn at the last minute, in fabric her mother Louise had chosen. Real white is for virgins, Louise had said, sly, vicious, in the tone she'd always reserved for Ana's father. Since his death, she only had Ana to use it on. And it had been Louise who took Ana's thick, wild hair and twisted it into a single, tight braid. As for Frank, his hair was slicked back, every hair in place, and he'd worn a tan polyester casual suit with an awful, green-leafed shirt.

In the wedding pictures, Ana's lips were pressed into a tight smile, chin tucked in, as if she was trying to disappear into the high-collared dress. Everything on Frank was lined up straight, like someone had laid a yardstick down his back. The hands came together at a point just around his groin, one hand clasped protectively over the other.

Before the marriage, Ana hadn't really known what she wanted. She had trained in lab work by default after college-it was something women could do, like nursing, teaching. Something to kill time until the right man came along. At the blood bank where she worked, she made deliveries, speeding everywhere, driving a cheap red Datsun from one hospital to the next. Blood-running. Her days were a drill of dashing from work to car to highway, to hospital labs, and on to the next round. She worked all night, drinking strong, black coffee to stay awake. She documented deliveries, scrawling notes in shaky letters and talking fast when the hospital called in the orders. She had driven the Datsun eighty miles an hour down the freeway, balancing the rushing of the blood inside her with the rush of the ride, billboard colors stretching outside the windows, flattening into amorphous streaks. She had never been with a man before Frank. Her life before had been ruled by her mother, and the church. And the church had made the position of God very clear. *The works of the flesh are these. Adultery, fornication, uncleanness, lasciviousness. They who do such things shall not inherit the kingdom of God.*

Ana washed her hands with disinfectant, trying to mask the hospital's smell-a nasty soup of iodine, floor soap, body fluids. She thought about Michael, about the way he had smiled at her. It was a kind smile, one that had stopped the frenzy of her work, if only for a minute. She wondered why a man would choose to be a nurse, would be willing to submit to the stares of those who thought it odd. She thought maybe he was like her, that he had done it to kill time, until something better came along. But maybe not. He looked like a man comfortable in his own skin. She turned off the light over the sink, wiped her hands. She thought about Emmy, imagined her waiting for her, fending off sleep until she got home. This was reason, at least, to finish up, to face the road.

2

She had to take the road in a rage of speed, just to get through the mud. It was slick, a river of sagging muck, cold brown hands that grabbed the Wagon and threatened to pull it under. She gripped the wheel, grinding forward, cursing Frank for failing to put down gravel, as he said he would.

Henry came out of his house, in time to check, to make sure she had shut the gate. She saw him dimly in the evening dusk, a hostile gremlin in the distance, bottle-thick glasses and wild red hair, and drove faster. If she hadn't shut it, he would have yelled at her until she was out of sight. She remembered the time he'd explained about the gate. He'd spoken slowly, as if she was a child incapable of understanding.

"To keep the weirdoes out," he said.

Ana had stared at his small, square teeth, set into an imitation smile. She waited for him to finish, then mumbled something about not having a key to the padlock. He pulled a ring of keys from his pocket, took one off, handed it to her. She'd started shutting the gate then, dutifully. It was too much to deal with–not worth it to resist.

The sight of Henry finally faded, and on the downside of the second hill, Ana headed into a skid. The Wagon lunged for the ditch and landed nose down, stuck, hopelessly. She got off the seatbelt and climbed out, unhurt, but shaky. She started the long wade home, her feet sinking with each step, ankle-high in the ooze. By the time she reached the hard-packed clay of the driveway, the mud on her feet had begun to dry to crust-like casts, weighing her down. She stamped up the stairs, opened the door.

Frank stared at her, inert in his chair. "Where the hell have you been?" It was all he really wanted to know. Not whether or not she was hurt, or needed help.

"I slid out," she said. "The Wagon's in the ditch."

"It was a crazy night," she added. "I got out late." She had gone crazy, or would, if he didn't stop looking at her that way.

He got up. "Shit."

"I'm sorry," she said.

"Yeah, right." He put on his coat, went for his keys.

In the quiet of the night Ana heard the scream of the winch as he worked, even from the living room where she sat on the piano bench, prying sticky lumps of clay from the laces on her tennis shoes, waiting for him. She could hear the Wagon being exhumed from the mire. She pulled the shoes off and went to watch for him from the kitchen window.

In the driveway, he fumbled with the cable, unhooking it from the trailer hitch, and something sprang loose. "Goddamit!" His hand jerked away and he shook it, wounded. He came back in a few minutes later, took a shower, came out to the kitchen and wrapped his hand in a dishtowel and ice. Ana lay on the sofa, still dressed.

"Are you coming to bed?" he asked.

"Yes," she said, wondering why she wasn't screaming at him, telling him how she blamed him, for everything. But instead she went to bed and found him reaching for her. When she gave in to him, it meant nothing. It was as if he reached in, searching for her heart, only to find the rock he'd built his house upon.

In the morning Ana watched him from the kitchen window. He stood in the driveway next to the pickup, staring at Margaret, their neighbor, who was moving deliberately, slowly, up the driveway. One fat braid, black and peppered with gray, hung over a woven poncho. She breathed heavily, every step labored, the feet in white deerskin boots that sparkled with cut glass beads. Frank stood with his arms folded, giving her his "keep your distance" look. Ana knew why. He didn't like Margaret. He didn't like her dogs, he didn't like her motor home. He didn't care that Ana admired her, just for surviving.

Margaret drew herself up. She faced him where he stood, planted like a rock. "Hey," she said, raising a hand to shield her eyes from the mid-day sun. "You brought a backhoe out the other day," she said.

"Yeah," Frank said. "So?"

"Any chance you could level out the road, up by my place?" She looked at him hard, square in the eye. "I'd pay you."

His chin tilted up, in stubborn response. "No," he said.

Ana moved to the door, opened it. "Hi," she said, interrupting, addressing herself to Margaret. She had to do something to stop Frank from acting the way he always did. "You're asking about the backhoe?"

"I want to get the road bladed," Margaret said. "Thought I could get some help."

Ana knew why. She had seen Margaret's purple Toyota the week before, swallowed whole by the mud in the road. Its headlights had winked at her from the ditch, but the rest of it was lost in the darkness, sinking into the slime. Likely, no one had helped her then, Ana thought. She'd probably had to dig the truck out with a shovel, prop it with a jack and some boulders, and extract it like a bad tooth with nothing but her own tough will and her two bare hands. And no one was going to help her now, either. That much was clear.

Frank's cold stare was now fixed on Ana, and she knew he wouldn't change his mind. But she realized, he didn't have to know she'd already heard his answer.

"We should be able to-" She stopped, feeling his eyes bore into her. She wasn't sure she was ready for this battle after all. And now she would have to give in, even before she'd started.

She turned her face to him, tried to convince him. "Couldn't you help? The road really does need work."

He shook his head. "No," he said. "It's Joe's backhoe."

There was a long, awkward silence. Ana knew what Margaret didn't know. She had already begged him to work on the road, and he'd said he would. No matter that it was his boss's backhoe, no matter Joe had told Frank he could use it as long as he needed it. She turned to Margaret, giving up, wanting to change the subject.

"Can you come inside?"

"Not today," Margaret said. "Got to get home to the animals."

"To the pack," Frank mumbled.

"What?" Margaret said. She glared back at him now.

"Nothing," he said. He cleared his throat, slapped the pickup hood in his own brand of "goodbye," then started for the stairs.

"Well," Margaret said. "Guess that's that. I'll come another time."

Frank let the door slam behind him.

"When *he's* not here," she added, shooting Ana a look that said, "What's his problem?" But she didn't say more. She just turned and rolled her body away slowly, the way it had come. It was as if she had some old injury, Ana thought. But she never knew Margaret to complain. In fact, Margaret barely talked at all. It must have taken a lot for her to come, to ask for help. But at least she did, at least she tried. When Ana pulled the door shut, she felt like a coward. Like a turtle retreating to its shell.

Frank followed her, closing the door with a deliberate flick of the latch. She could feel him behind her, waiting for her to meet his eyes. She didn't want to.

"*The road really does need work,*" he said in a woman's voice, mimicking her. His eyebrows were cocked up high, digging narrow furrows into the long, stern forehead. He waited for an explanation.

Ana raised her eyes only halfway. "Her truck gets stuck up there every week."

"Not my problem. Besides, she smells like all those dogs she has. Don't ever want to be that close to her again."

Ana felt her throat closing in on itself, knowing it was time for her to be silent, to apologize. But she didn't want to. Margaret had to struggle for basic necessities, water, warmth, a decent road to travel.

"She probably doesn't have enough water for baths," she said.

As far as Ana was concerned, Margaret could smell however she wanted to, could bring home a hundred animals. She deserved some respect for facing up to Frank, without flinching, even once.

His eyes were still on her, pinning her. "She's Indian," he said. "Doesn't believe in baths."

Ana turned away, letting him have the last word, again. There was no use in arguing. There never was. She was glad she had to leave for work, glad to have an excuse to get away. She couldn't stand to look at Frank for one more minute. She went to the bedroom, grabbed her coat and purse.

"You're leaving early today," he said.

"Change of shift," she said, avoiding his eyes.

He reached for a cigar, flicked the lighter, inhaled smoke. He'd done just that, Ana thought, when she had gone into labor with Emmy. The beginning had been hard-a grinding pain that grabbed and held on, turning and twisting.

"It's the baby," she'd said, shaking Frank awake. The cramping went on, a slow, pendulous rhythm.

He had sat up halfway, propping himself on an elbow and reaching for a cigar. "What?" he asked.

She nodded. "We need to go to the hospital."

"How long since the labor started?" He flicked his lighter and the flame shot up. He drew in smoke, then let it out of his lips in a steady gray stream.

It didn't matter how long it had been, she'd thought, already angry. But she answered, dutifully, turning her head so she wouldn't have to breathe in smoke. "Fifteen minutes, maybe."

"I'm going to time them," he said, propping his watch up on the bedside table. "Tell me when you have the next one." He took a long drag on the cigar and leaned back into the pillows. The smell of it disgusted her, made her want to throw up. This was so like Frank. Not the frantic Dick Van Dyke of the TV shows she'd watched as a kid, the clumsy father-to-be, rushing nervously around, bags packed for the hospital, disoriented, semi-hysterical. No, not Frank. He'd finished the cigar and put it out. He drifted in and out of sleep while she waited for each pain to come and go.

After an hour, convinced the labor was real, he had gathered her into the Wagoneer, and the long, torturous drive had begun. One long ripping pain seized her and lasted the length of the road. The cramping arrested her, crushed her with every jolt of the car against ruts and boulders. She had been panting and covered in sweat, and when it ended, they had passed the "It'll

Do Motel," the adobe church at *Cañoncito*, the cemetery, the junk car lot, the Laundromat. They were already on the highway. The headlights cast a dim beacon through gauzy fog, the serpentine highway loping beneath them, pale, yellow, hypnotic. Only when she saw the white lights of Santa Fe, a strip of diamonds below the *Sangre de Cristos*, had she realized it. The labor had stopped.

She hadn't told him. She hadn't been able to face the idea of having to go home, back up the road, the slamming pain every time wheels hit rock. She hadn't wanted to think of what the doctors would say, much less Frank. She had willed the labor, with all her might, to start again. And miraculously, it had, as if the child had been listening, and though not quite ready, decided to make the journey. For her mother's sake.

On her way to work, Ana let the Wagon crawl, taking it slow as Frank had said. At least the mud had dried out a little, and the four-wheel drive managed to churn its way through. But still, she was exhausted with the effort of it before she ever reached the hospital. In the lab she slammed a cup of coffee down, steeled herself for the long night ahead, and carried orders for the psych ward, crossing the speckled linoleum to the elevator. Before she could get in, the steel doors opened, slid shut, opened, then slid and locked again. The controls were jammed. She'd have to take the stairs. They were narrow and so steep she had to go straight up, straining her calf muscles. When she stepped out to the ward, catching her breath, she could smell the sickness already, urine, vomit. She saw Michael there, throwing soiled linens into hampers, scribbling notes in the logbook. When he saw her, he stopped and faced her squarely.

"I just called you," he said.

Ana stood back, waiting. She wondered why he looked at her so intently, as if he knew her well.

"Oh-" she said, fidgeting, rearranging the things in her tray.

"Room thirty-six-B," he said. Heroin addict."

She avoided his eyes, hurried to the room he directed her to. Her face felt warm when he looked at her. The door to the room was ajar, and he walked to it, held it for her.

"A Chem Survey," he said, looking after her as she walked in. Not a big hurry, but they need it in an hour or two."

"Okay," Ana said, looking to the woman in the bed before her. She was obese, eyes darting like animals in a fire. She had seen Ana coming.

Shards of sweaty hair fell across a pink, swollen face.

"You can't do it," she said. "No veins."

"I have to." Ana glanced back to the door, looking for Michael, but by now he was gone. She put the tourniquet and syringe on the bed.

"Holy Jee-sus," the woman said, shaking her head. She looked defeated for just one minute, but then she reached back to untie the strings of her hospital gown. Before Ana could protest, a massive chest heaved before her.

The woman traced a pale blue vein on one of her breasts, with her finger. The nail was chewed back to the quick, only a smudge of red nail polish surviving. "Take it," she said. "Or leave it."

"Any other good veins?" Ana asked.

"Nope," the woman said. She grinned. It was a lovely set of teeth, but for one chipped incisor.

Ana took one of the great arms, though gently. She wrapped a tourniquet around it, and it made a deep seam of flesh. There was one fat vein in the crook of the elbow, but it was hard. It rolled away when Ana touched it. She tried the other arm, and the ankles. All the veins were tough, used up. For the first time, she took the woman seriously. She picked up the syringe, showed it to her. "This won't work with that vein," she said. "Or this," she gestured limply with the tourniquet. It was her turn to feel defeated.

"I'll hold it for you," the woman said. She cupped the breast in both hands, pushing against it. The vein plumped up under the skin, curling, tender, like an earthworm. Ana shook her head in disbelief.

She searched through her equipment, rearranging the clutter. There was a tiny needle, one she used for babies. She uncapped it and slipped it, easily, into the vein. Maroon-colored blood ran into the syringe, thick, slow.

"I can't believe it," Ana said, more to herself than the woman.

"Blood out of a turnip," she said, running one fat-fingered hand through her hair.

Ana pressed cotton into the pale flesh. "Hold this a minute," she said.

One last time she studied the scarred arms. "You should give those veins a rest."

"Sure," the woman said, shrugging as if she didn't mean it. But she kept grinning, the smile perfect but for that one chipped tooth.

Ana bit her tongue. There was no point in lecturing. And besides, who was she to judge? The woman had kept this one vein, this one sacred thing. That was something. She pressed the bandage on, checked it before leaving. When she turned to the door this time, Michael was there, watching her.

"You're back," she said.

"Did you need me?" He looked guilty for abandoning her, but still, he was smiling, teasing her.

"A little," she said. "But I got it. Twenty cc's. Turnip blood."

"You did good," he said, gesturing for Ana to follow him. "Can you take a break for a minute?"

"Sure," she said, but she wasn't sure. Not at all. She didn't know why he was so kind to her. She put the tray down hesitantly, stopping to scrub her hands in the sink. She looked up, caught sight of herself in the mirror. Her hair was frazzled, eyes bloodshot. She knew what her mother-or Frank-would say about his kindness. That he wanted something. That she should stay away. But it seemed he was willing her to stay. He was filling an electric kettle with water, offering her tea.

"I'm sorry I didn't stay to help you," he said.

"It's okay," she said, suddenly shy again, avoiding his eyes.

He passed her a cup and a teabag, and she studied the cup to keep from looking at him. It was thick-walled pottery, almost egg-shaped, with fire cracks streaking through a shining brown. It was heavy, a handful of earth, turned and golden.

"You like it?" he asked.

"That's beautiful," she said, and she meant it. "Where did you get it?"

"I made it." He shrugged, as if it was nothing.

"How?" Ana was taken off guard. He was so different. Not the sort of man she'd ever met before.

"Just your garden variety pottery. You could do it."

"Oh no-not me," Ana said.

"Yes, you," he said. "I could teach you."

In spite of herself, Ana's mind began to turn on the idea of learning this new thing. From him.

He ran his fingers around the rim of the cup. "See how this isn't even? The Japanese call this *shibui*, the flaw that makes something beautiful. The shape has to have some room, some freedom."

Ana shivered. He was only standing, waiting for her to say something. But she couldn't speak, not even when he turned to lift the kettle, then back to her, pouring hot water over tea. She drank, warming her hands on the cup, keeping her eyes down, waiting for him to speak again, so she wouldn't have to.

"Like with people," he said, and she nodded.

There was a sort of electricity in her body, like the fire cracks shooting through the round of the cup. It sparked in the sight of his fingers, his eyes, his hair that was bound at the nape of his neck with that same red braided cloth. Steam rose to her lips from the cup, the tea smelling of cardamom, of honey.

3

At home, Ana sat down at the piano, got the sheet music out, ran her fingers along the keys. The piano was a mahogany Chickering, an old-fashioned upright her father had given her, hopelessly out of tune, even worse than the one at Tino's. Three or four of the keys were broken. They made a dull thunk, but she worked around them.

Emmy stirred and rubbed her eyes. "Sing," she said. She rolled to the center of the couch, folding her knees beneath her, waiting. Ana obeyed, leaning into the keyboard as she played. But her voice was tense, stifled, not like she knew it should be. Not for a song like this.

"One of these mornings, you're goin to rise up singing. Then you'll spread your wings, and you'll take to the sky..."

She heard Frank coming back and stopped, her fingers falling from the keys. There was the familiar rocking of the wooden steps, uneven, the heels of his steel-toed boots digging in against the gritty ice. He opened the door.

"Why'd you stop playing?"

"No reason." She fidgeted with her hair, picking at the ends.

Now Emmy was wide awake. She threw herself onto Frank's back, latching her arms around his neck in a stranglehold. He reached back to tickle her, and she squirmed to avoid his hands. He pinned her against his side, teasing her neck and feet, and she surrendered, shrieking with laughter.

Ana ignored the game. She had other things on her mind. "Can we get a Christmas tree soon?"

"No. Not til a week before Christmas. They get too dried out if you get them too soon." His jaw set into a stiff, hard line.

She wanted to argue, but held back. She knew he wouldn't give in. She watched as he rummaged through clutter, found whatever nut or bolt he'd been looking for, and walked out again. The front door clapped shut, the glass panels rattling in the aluminum frame.

Emmy ran to Ana, clutching at her legs. "Dance with me!"

Ana stood, swung her around once, and slipped her softly onto the floor.

"Dance with Dooby."

"He's sleeping."

Ana almost laughed at her-the droopy eyes, fighting to stay open, one braid intact, the other held by a pink rubber band. "That's what you should be doing."

"I'm not sleepy."

Ana carried her, still wriggling, to the bedroom. She sat with Emmy until she fell asleep, one chubby hand gripping the monkey by one of his black-button eyes. She thought again about Christmas, about the tree. Frank would never agree to get one until he'd decided the time was right. She felt hopeless about it, depressed. But it wasn't only Frank. It was something about her childhood that was making her sad, about how things had been, and how she'd wanted them to be. It was her father she missed, since his death. He was the one who had rescued the little plastic reindeer and sleigh from the garbage. Her mother had thrown them out after one of the preachers had said Santa Claus was an idol. A false god. He hadn't said what her mother really thought, though. Louise filled that in later. It was a thing like Catholics worshipped-Catholics, like Ana's father. A pagan.

Ana went to stand on the wooden steps outside the front door. The night was dark, cold, and the stars hung bright and low. She wanted to remember a better Christmas. A tree with lights on it, the sleigh and reindeer beneath it. She wanted to see her father. He used to tell her funny stories in his thick Cajun accent, teasing her about the Loup-Garou, the great wolf of the forest. How that wolf would steal her away if she wouldn't be a good girl and go to sleep. She felt a stab of loneliness, bitterness.

Only one idea came to her, of how to make up for it. Maybe she could get a tree on her own. She could keep it behind the house. Frank had a chainsaw she could use. But she realized that was hopeless. He kept the saw locked in a room at the back of the house. And besides, she didn't know how to use it. She opened the door, went back inside, stoked the fire. The logs had gone to smoldering, the flames dying out. She couldn't revive them. She gave up, put the poker away, dusted ash from her hands. She decided to stop thinking about the holidays. There was enough to worry about, without having to talk Frank into something he didn't want to do. She would stop thinking about it, let him get a tree when he was ready.

In the morning, she gathered laundry that had been put off for too long. It was Saturday and all the clothes were filthy, Emmy's pants, mud-smeared and damp, jean-cuffs crusted and stiff. They had to be washed before Monday, before she had to work again. She piled everything into the Wagon-soap, bleach, four loads of laundry stuffed into pillowcases. Emmy made her wait, twisting the top of a pillowcase she'd been hoarding things in. Secret things. Ana had seen some of it-a set of old keys with a black leather fob and a medallion with an "R" etched into it, a jar of pennies, some crumbled animal crackers. Ana didn't know what it was for. Emmy gave only a cryptic answer when quizzed about it. "For camping," she said, and she would say no more. But the collection grew every day, with new things found in Ana's bureau, from under sofa cushions, from the backs of dusty cabinets. Emmy stuffed the pillowcase under her bed, deliberately, then grabbed Dooby and trotted outside to the Wagon.

Ana didn't worry about whatever Emmy was up to. She could always find her near the back of the house, in one of her not-so-secret hiding places, talking out loud to Dooby, or to herself. She'd be explaining something, about what birds liked to eat, about how juniper berries tasted, about why she wasn't allowed to go down the road by herself. She wriggled into her back seat, her faded tennis shoes gaping open, their shoelaces limp, undone. Ana buckled the seat belt around her, pulling it snug. They would have to brave the road together.

This time, it wasn't so bad. The sun had dried it even more, to fudge-like slabs that were possible to navigate, and except for a turn of wheel-churning in the pit, they pulled through. At the village Laundromat, they found their way through the heavy glass door, through a fog of bleach-smelling air. They walked past metal benches bolted to concrete floors, past the portholes of the whirring dryers. Ana stuffed the laundry into the washers, dropping in quarters, adding soap. When the last load was in, she listened to the hum of the dryers and the hushed voices of the *abuelitas*. Their salty-black hair was bunched and knotted at the backs of their necks, their faces leathery, like dried-apple skin. They leaned crooked backs over well-behaved granddaughters, fussing with the childrens' black braids that wound like new rope around rosy, angelic faces. Unlike them, Emmy was wriggling and suddenly obsessed with the need for a quarter. She pulled on Ana's shirt, whining. There was a white plastic chicken in a Plexiglas box. A quarter would make the chicken cluck, spin around, and shoot out one of its yellow or green prize eggs. Ana gave her two quarters, and Emmy grinned and plugged them in.

"Come on," Ana said, helping her carry two green eggs, leading her to a cramped bathroom at the back of the building. Her mission was to scrub the sap out of Emmy's hair. It took a long time, Emmy trying to escape, Ana working on the sticky clumps with soap and water and a broad-toothed comb. Fifteen minutes later, they opened the bathroom door to a waiting line of annoyed *abuelitas*.

"Sorry," Ana said. "*Lo Siento.*"

"*De nada,*" they said, but they stared after her with darting eyes, accusing. She hurried Emmy past them to get the wet clothes into the dryers. She was strange to them, Ana was sure. She lived in their world, but apart, different, rich compared to them, a *gringa*. Her blue jeans, her curly brown hair. Her child that didn't mind. "*Como es travieso!*" she heard them say. Naughty girl. Still, she thought, she *meant* to be different. She didn't want to use a Laundromat. She was looking forward to getting the washer and dryer Frank had promised. He'd gotten a raise. He would buy them soon. He'd install them in the nook at the back of the kitchen, and then the laundry would be easy. Emmy helped her fold the clothes after they were washed and finally dry. Ana carried them in piles to the Wagon, letting the heavy glass door of the Laundromat snap shut behind her. "Hurry," she said to Emmy. "I've got to get to work."

She heard the old women whispering, sharing their local *periodico*.

"*Se murio, pobresita,*" said one. "Jose, he was drunk, he didn't even go to the *hospitál* with her."

The others responded in unison. "*Borracho!*"

Ana watched them working as she put the key in the Wagon's ignition. They hoisted great white sheets like sails in brown-spotted hands, walking together, joining the corners, folding the sheets precisely, like ceremonial flags. Next to her, in the parking lot, their bare-metal jalopies were loaded with pumpkins and winter squash, alfalfa. She envied the women. She imagined climbing into the back of one of their rusty trucks and running away. She and Emmy could be like stowaways, riding one of the rutted roads of the valley to a smoke-filled *casita*. They could hole up there for the winter, help them plant their gardens in the spring. But for now, it was hopeless to think of running away. For now, there was laundry, and work, and Frank.

When she drove up the road, back to the house, she heard something that gave her a start. Then she smiled. It was a long, high-pitched whine, the sound of steel on wood, coming from Margaret's place. It was a chainsaw. Margaret had a chainsaw. A saw that could cut a Christmas tree. Next week, she thought, she might borrow it. She might cut a Christmas tree herself, if Frank didn't want to. It was a little crazy, she knew. But she was suddenly pleased with herself, happy to have thought of it. She kissed Emmy good night when she left that evening, jangling the car keys in her fingers. A Christmas tree, she thought, and smiled. She hit the gas hard, realizing what she hadn't before-that Frank might not even have to know.

4

na told Frank she was planning to visit her mother in Albuquerque, bringing it up just before the weekend. "She's been begging to see Emmy," she said. "Just two days."

"I'll think about it," he said.

She hadn't been asking his permission, but now she saw that it was required.

"She'll just make you both go to church," he said.

"I know." Ana twisted her hands, hoping he would agree. "But I want to see her anyway."

He looked as if he was struggling to think of another reason to disapprove. "What am I supposed to do while you're over there?" he asked.

"It won't be that long," she said. "I'll leave early tomorrow, so I can get back on Sunday afternoon."

He had not given permission. She slipped into the bedroom and searched the closet for an overnight bag, packing quickly, hoping he wouldn't say more.

"All right then," he said. "Just a few days." He was scowling, but he seemed to resign himself to her decision.

Ana was grateful, for once, for Louise's influence. She could be annoying when she didn't get her way.

In the morning she got Emmy ready as planned, and headed out.

Frank stood at the door as she drove away, looking forlorn, abandoned. Ana didn't care. She was tired of his constant attention. Even Louise would be a relief.

When they arrived in Albuquerque, Louise opened the door of her split-level stucco, the only one of its kind in a "too rich" neighborhood, as Ana's father, before he died, had always put it. The garden in the back was orderly as ever, clean and trimmed back. In the summer, the squash grew there, heavy as bowling balls, red tomatoes, *chiles*. It had always been the best garden on the block. "You can't get anything this good at the grocery," her mother would say when her father said they didn't really need a garden. "Those store things are dirty or spoiled," she always said. "No thank you. I'll keep my garden. When I'm dead, you can put me there, for fertilizer." She'd said it so many times, Ana stopped eating the vegetables. The garden made her think of death-rot, seeping out of the tomatoes and squash, served up on the Formica table in the kitchen, the crimson and yellow blood staining Louise's precious Blue Willow china.

Louise had all the material things she'd ever wanted. Central heating. Plush pink carpet. Cut glass on mirrored shelves, ceramic birds, music boxes, spoons in little wooden cabinets, pictures of the family in antique oval frames. Bric-a-brac on every surface. And there was a full refrigerator, but much of the food in it was disgusting–canned meat, angel-food cake, fruit punch.

Emmy made herself at home, plowing an old doll carriage she found in the attic into every downstairs corner, loud and fast, yipping like an untrained puppy. She made an hour-long tour of the den, kitchen, and dining room. There was a near miss with the china hutch–it pitched and rocked and the Blue Willow rattled, and Ana held her breath, waiting for the crash. But there was no disaster, only what looked like the aftermath of one, in the bed of the carriage. A porcelain baby doll Ana used to have, with the dinner Emmy had tried to feed it: jelly bread, a crumbled Oreo.

Ana almost laughed out loud. For her, that doll had been untouchable. She'd tried, as a child, to play with it. But her mother had always reminded her of the rules: "Be careful," she'd say. "It's fragile." Then she'd try to act like it didn't matter. "Don't put it away," she'd say. "I got it for you to play with." Now it was Emmy's turn, and she was standing the rules on their heads. By the time she'd exhausted herself, the precious doll was missing a foot, and one of its glass eyes was stuck shut with peanut butter.

Ana scanned the pictures on the wall above the kitchen table. One in particular caught her eye. It was a photograph of herself as a child, standing alone on the clipped green lawn of the church. She stood tall and straight-faced, her little girl's legs pressed together, black patent-leather shoes flat on the ground. Her hair was yanked back into long, tight braids, and she wore the new dress her mother had made for her, starched, yellow and white cotton, with a smocked bodice and puffy sleeves. Louise had spent hours smocking that bodice; it was as if the stiff little dress bound Ana up, bolstered her. It was as if without the dress, she might fly apart, or disappear. Only one thing gave away her distress. One small hand held a button and twisted, so hard that the smocking was all bunched up, and the edge of the lacy white slip showed just above the knees. Ana remembered why she did it. She thought if she twisted hard enough, someone would notice. If they noticed, maybe they would let her go home, go back to her room, pull the covers over her head, and not have to hear her parents shouting. What had they fought about? She didn't remember.

The fighting, she remembered. It had never seemed to end. It was always at night when she should have been sleeping. She used to stand at the top of the stairs, squeezing her eyes shut and pressing her hands against her ears until she could hear only the rushing of the blood in her head. When the noise wedged in even through that, she ran outside, her thin cotton nightgown flapping around her knees, throwing herself on the grass in the back yard, crying to get their attention. No one heard her, tried to stop her. Eventually, her throat would begin to hurt and she would go back inside, lying in bed for a long time before she slept, feeling a thickness in her chest that lasted all night and into the morning.

Even as a child, she had tried to understand it. As far as she could tell, all their fighting was about how her mother thought she was too good for her father, that his rise into management hadn't made up for the fact that he had come from a family of sharecroppers. He would never really amount to more than that. Never mind that her mother's family had been poorer than his had. At least they were "regular Americans" with a home of their own. Ana knew her parents' marriage wasn't what it should be. The "obey" part was more or less there, but her mother hadn't seemed to know the meaning of "love" or "honor." Louise said she wished she had never gotten married. She had been bitter, and the bitterness turned to a rage that suffocated them all, on car trips, in the living room, at the dinner table. It withered Ana's spirit. When her father had the heart attack, Ana had driven them both to the hospital. They'd gotten there too late. But Louise hadn't cried. Not one tear.

Ana hadn't complained about the suffering of the family. She learned to keep quiet, to tie up whatever reckless feelings worked themselves loose, to keep them twined together, under control. Even now, she sat, hands folded limply on her lap, waiting for Emmy to wear herself out. A television blared from the next room, a radio program with a familiar sermon.

"How great our God is! How merciful! Jesus promises us that if we sacrifice our lives for his sake, we will save it eternally!"

"I'm so glad we're going to church together tomorrow," Louise chirped.

Ana wasn't glad, but there was, like with Frank, no point in arguing.

On Sunday they dropped Emmy off in the children's room. The crowd pushed in from all directions, strangers she used to see every week, without fail. Their faces pressed in on her, the antiseptic-smelling mouths grinning obscenely, excruciatingly close. It was all too familiar.

"Ana!" someone barked from across the corridor. It was Jerry, from her old Sunday School class. He hadn't changed at all. His brown eyes shone like his slicked-back hair, and his smile was sincere, his stubby, wide-set teeth agog. The church had been Jerry's refuge, compared with the torture of public schools. Here, at least, they mocked him behind his back. It hadn't helped when he asked his favorite question, which he never got an answer to: "Teacher, what's "for-ni-*ca*-tion?"

"Never mind..." the teacher had muttered, barely containing her disgust, and the class giggled behind their hands.

Now he reached his spindly arms out to Ana and grabbed her, hugging her too close.

"Welcome home, Ana! Welcome back! Come home where you belong! This is where you belong!"

Ana tried to think of what she should say. She'd promised herself not to be fake, despite her aggravation at having to be here again. But she didn't want to hurt his feelings.

"Thanks," she said. "It's good to see you too." She patted his back, then pushed him away when he wouldn't let go, gently, but with insistent hands. She felt the boniness of his chest, the urgent breath that came from him when she finally had to shove him away and lock her elbows against him.

"How nice that you're here!" another parishioner exclaimed, and Ana tried to escape from that one too. She wanted to say it was not nice to be here. This wasn't where she belonged. She belonged in the hospital with the crazy kid who didn't fit in, like her. She belonged in the nurse's lounge, talking of pottery, pouring tea. She belonged any place but here. But she put on a good face, lied, nodded for the others who crowded in, patting her back and her face, gushing.

She spotted a woman she remembered well. Once, she had squirmed on the hard, wooden pews, aching from the long hours of sitting still. She could still hear the woman's sniping: "Why can't they control that child?"

The man next to her had never answered. He only stared blankly at the preacher, pretending not to hear. Ana's eyes fell on him now, remembering that she thought well of him for ignoring the woman's insults. She thought he might help her once, when she was eleven. Brother Roberts, a leader, they said. He might talk to her parents.

"They argue all the time," she'd said.

He looked nervous, as if his collar was too tight. His face turned suddenly red, his eyes shifting from her face to a place over her head, at the far end of the room.

"I'm not sure what you'd like me to do," he said.

"I just thought–I don't know," Ana said. She wondered if she'd said something wrong.

"You need to pray," he said, and from then on, Ana knew, there was no "brother," no man of God, or God, for that matter, to help her.

She closed her eyes. She couldn't concentrate on the service.

She tried not to think about how miserable the young girl in the pew in front of her looked, squirming in her seat, the parents pinching her, sniping at her to settle down. Louise signaled to Ana to take the communion tray. She took it meekly, but when she raised the drink to her mouth, it tasted like blood, almost bitter. Ana thought of how much Louise had devoted her life to this. She remembered her mother scouring the Bible over and over again, searching for assurance that she was better than all others, that she would find reward for her suffering in heaven.

"I hope you're not working too much," Louise said, driving them back to the house.

Ana didn't answer right away, and when she finally did, her voice was strained. "I'm not."

"That's good. Men don't like to be left alone while their women work."

"I'm only working a few days a week," Ana said. She was glad, already, to think of going home. Her mother was trying to drive her insane.

"I didn't know. I wonder sometimes. You seem unhappy." Louise was pulling up to the house, maneuvering the car into the garage.

"I'm all right," Ana said. There was no point in confessing to Louise that she was right-that the struggle with Frank was tiresome, intolerable.

"Are you sure?" Louise got out of the car, flicked a switch for the electric garage door opener, waited while it groaned upward.

Ana sighed. She thought of telling her, of looking for sympathy. Surely she could muster some support, given her sour view on marriage.

"Things aren't easy between Frank and me," she said. She wondered what more would be safe to say. Things were never safe with her mother.

"Well, things weren't always easy for me with your father, either," Louise said. One eyebrow lifted, almost imperceptibly.

"I know," Ana said. It was as she'd thought. There would be only judgment, again, a sermon. There would be no sympathy, after all.

"You have responsibilities," Louise said. She turned off the car and waited while Ana got Emmy out of the booster seat.

Ana sighed. There was no point in arguing about it. She would just have to hear, once again, the lecture on the duty of a woman, the rights of a man. "I know, Mama."

"You're mad?" Louise unfolded her arms. "I'm just saying-"

"Don't worry about it. I'm just tired. I'm going to lie down in Daddy's old room. Could you watch Emmy?" She had to get away from her, before she exploded. She didn't want to argue.

"Of course," Louise said. "You go rest. You'll feel better."

Ana stuffed an answer back to the bottom of her throat. She wouldn't feel better. There was no place to feel better. Not here, not with Frank, not anywhere. She went upstairs as she'd said, to the room where her father had stayed until he built a place at the lake to get away. His treasured old record player was there, heavy as an anvil, a thick brass arm with a needle that had to be screwed in by hand. His records were still in the closet, along with snapshots, of fish he'd caught, of relatives long dead, of the village where he was born.

She noticed a poster he'd hung there years ago, just before he began to go quiet. It was a picture of Chief Joseph, with high cheekbones and sad eyes, like her father. At the bottom, it read: *I am tired of fighting. My heart is sad and sick. From where the sun now stands, I will fight no more forever.*

She knew it was about her mother, about their marriage. She remembered her father standing openly against Louise in only one battle, over a kitten Ana desperately wanted. And he had won, too. When he gave it to her, she cried into its dusty fur, making herself sneeze, then fell asleep to its ragged purring.

She read the words on the poster again, knowing her father had given up everything her mother didn't approve of: the soft-sounding language he could only speak with relatives, the land he'd wanted to farm, the old Catholic rites. It was hard for Ana to remember those things. Mostly, she remembered the way he died. The heart attack, his body swollen and gray, no longer the small but solid man who had always made her feel so safe. She started packing the records into her suitcase. She pulled the record player out, made sure the latches were secure. These things would go with her. She needed them, to remind herself.

5

At the hospital the lab orders were piled up, and Ana raced from one patient to the next. Everything seemed to get in the way of what she needed to do-the clutter of blood pressure cuffs, crutches, bedpans.

"*Dame su brazo,*" she said to her first patient, a tiny *vieja,* listless, unresisting. "*Necesito sacar un poquito de sangre.*" The woman surrendered her wrinkled, brown arm. Ana labeled the tubes, carried the blood to the lab. One year to live, or less, the tech said. For the tattooed biker later that night, six months, if he was lucky. The techs made bets on these things, sometimes, and they were usually right. Ana cringed at the muzak on the intercom, droning tonelessly. "*We Wish You a Merry Christmas,*" the singers crooned, in time to squealing gurneys, suction tubes, the blip of monitors.

She noticed Michael in the psych ward, his back turned, the lean, corded muscles of his arms as they reached for a chart on the wall. Tonight, seeing him again made her feel flustered, nervous. She told herself she should get out before he tried to talk to her, should get back to the lab, back to work. But before she could escape, he called to her.

"Come to Tino's after work?" he asked. The lines in his forehead gathered in a nervous frown.

Ana's heart tumbled. Yes, she thought. Yes. But then she thought of Frank, of the price she would have to pay if she went. "No orders?" she asked, stalling for time. "No heroin addicts tonight?"

"No orders," he said, looking more nervous than ever. "Just Tino's." Ana didn't think he looked like someone who'd deliberately planned to ask a married woman for her company. He looked innocent, earnest. How could she say no? She weighed her options. What excuse would she have? She didn't feel like dealing with whatever Frank had to say. On the other hand, there were all those nights she'd gone straight home, dutifully. And there were the times he'd left her at home, alone with Emmy. An hour after work at Tino's shouldn't be such a big deal. But it was. She knew it was.

"I'd better not," she said.

"Please." His eyes were on hers. He wasn't smiling. He was serious, looking earnest. Searching. "Just for a while."

"I'll think about it," she said. She laughed, mostly at herself. She was being silly to think so much of the invitation. It was just the usual nurse's ritual, the evening at Tino's. Nothing personal. But she rolled it over and over in her mind as she went through her rounds, hurrying, finishing early.

It was personal, she could see it in his eyes. Then she decided. She *would* go to Tino's. She would be there early, to see him. Before anyone else.

When she was there and waiting, a small coalition from the ER arrived, joining her in the cloud of smoke, pulling chairs back from the beer-smelling bar. They were drunk within the hour. They pulled out the piano bench and pushed her onto it, and didn't stop harassing her until she agreed to play. "Do *Auld Lang Syne*," they demanded. She obeyed, singing along with them, laughing at the off-key voices stumbling through the refrains, tripping over half-forgotten words. She started on the Christmas songs she knew by heart, *Joy to the World, O Come Ye Merry Gentlemen, Jingle Bells,* then played a song her mother used to sing, *Yellow Rose of Texas,* and a hush filled the room.

She was singing alone when Michael appeared, at last. He didn't join the crowd, but stood at the doorway, listening. She kept singing, keeping her foot on the pedal until the last tinny note of the piano faded into quiet.

Then there was a burst of raucous applause, and Michael pried her loose from the crowd, pulled out a chair for her. They sat with a pitcher of beer between them, talking for two hours, about the headlines that scrolled on the soundless television at the back of the bar. Bush and Cheney. Hurricanes. Global warming. Terrorists. Ana studied the pale amber light of the beer, feeling a soft blurriness, a growing affection for the world and all its woes, for Michael, for the sweet, sad helplessness of it all.

"America's screwed," he said.

"True," she agreed. But she was distracted from what they had been discussing. She was noticing that the gold in his eyes matched the fire cracks in his pottery. That his hands made pictures when he told a story, that he listened to her when she talked, not like Frank.

She tried to focus. She had to be clear, had to stop thinking about the way he was leaning toward her, so close, the way his knees were almost touching hers under the wobbly bar table.

"It has to change," he said, and his words seemed laden with some other meaning, something not at all about the nation, the world. It sounded more private, more tender, like something they hadn't been talking about at all.

He studied her. "You're smiling," he said. "That's good."

She laughed.

"What's so funny?" He smiled too, and his knee bumped hers. "Nothing," she said. She realized she needed to sober up, to go home.

"You're tough to figure," he said.

"I know."

"So who are you, really, Ana? It was no idle question. His eyes were locked on hers, and she couldn't look away.

What could she tell him? She had already confessed that she was a wife, a mother. If there was more to say, what use was it? Yet he didn't turn away from her. It didn't frighten him.

"Who knows?" she said.

"Are you so complicated?" he asked. The frown in his forehead was back, and she pitied him, his misfortune in meeting her.

"I guess so." There was more to her than she cared to say. There was the fact that she was married to someone, but she no longer felt it in her heart.

"Why?" he asked.

"I just am," she said. "Complicated."

He leaned toward her again. "Complicated, but beautiful."

Her heart skipped, and she searched the table, the pitcher of beer, any place her eyes could find to rest, except on his. They were too full of some sudden, irrational infatuation, and she felt it too. She was terrified. It had to stop.

She pushed her chair back, trying to start the process of leaving.

"Coffee first," he said. "Nurse's orders."

"Yes, first," she said. He was right, after all.

They ordered the coffee and she added too much sugar. She watched the way his hair escaped its bindings, the way it fell across one temple, curled and wildly out of place.

"I really have to go soon," she said. She thought of Frank and Emmy, waiting.

"Not yet," he said.

"I have to," she said.

"You shouldn't drive," he said. His eyes never faltered. He waited, still, for her to look at him, straight on, as he had looked at her since the moment they met.

"I'm fine," she said. Fine as a wicked woman could be. She tried to sound like she was telling the truth. She was okay to drive, but she wasn't fine. Her legs felt weak. It was crazy. He was crazy. He didn't know her. She didn't know him.

"Stay," he said. "Please. Just for a while." His hand reached across the table, took her hand, pressed it.

"I can't. Really," she said.

"Do you work tomorrow?" he asked. She could see him yielding to her will, though reluctantly. When she stood up, he stood, helped her into her coat. He pressed the palm of his hand into her back, protectively, waiting for her answer.

"Yes," she said. She didn't want to go home, to see Frank, to smell his cigars, to hear the steady drone his breath made as he slept.

"I come in at three," she said, and pried herself away. She drove home, thinking about how she would borrow Margaret's saw and cut a Christmas tree, Frank be damned. And she would find the plastic reindeer and she would be happy again, and she wouldn't be drinking beer and thinking about other things that should not be thought of. Her legs would stop feeling weak and she would be strong to hold Emmy even if she was very, very tired, even if she thought right now that she would never be that strong again.

In the morning, Ana opened her eyes to a dusty light. She heard the sound of Frank's white pickup as he started it. He would rev the engine and back out of the driveway like always, heading out past La Cueva to get to Joe Dowell's construction company. He worked as a foreman, ordering the Mexican immigrant workers around. He made plenty of money, it was true. But it wasn't like he had said it would be. A nice house, the good life. They could have afforded to finish the house, to get the road fixed. But he insisted on doing it all himself. "Better that way," he said, and there was no winning if Ana tried to argue. Now, though, her only worry was waiting for him to go to work, so she could follow through on her plan. She pulled the window curtains back, watched the truck grind out of the driveway, the usual snarl of jumper cables, rope, and a winch slapping against the bed. Frank's prized Winchester was mounted solidly in the rear window, like a trophy, like the final defense against any threat. She waited until she heard the engine grind once more as he navigated the dip, then the clanks and bangs when he made it over the last hill. He was finally gone.

She slipped into jeans and a sweatshirt and got Emmy up, who groggily insisted on wearing the same clothes she'd worn for the last three days, a long stretchy top with hot-pink flowers and tights, jaybird blue. Then Emmy was wide awake, scuttling behind Ana like a sand crab, all arms and legs marching, dancing, everything moving three times as fast as it needed to in order to climb the short stretch of road to Margaret's place.

There was the motor home, the word "Eagle" painted on the side, the red script faded, chipped. The thing was an eyesore, with its broad, flat windows, curtained all around, hunkered down in its homemade siding. But Margaret made it clear to anyone who cared to ask that she wasn't the type to live in a normal house, wasn't the type to have any company who would care. Ana had only visited once before, when they'd first moved out to La Cueva. Then Frank had said he didn't want her taking Emmy there. "Too dirty," he said.

It was true, things were rough at Margaret's place. Pipes ran from the motor home into a green-black sewage pond. Weeds sprouted like cabbage from its pungent, brackish soup. At the side of the driveway, there was a chain link fence. A gray hound snuffled behind it, his whole rump wagging. Beyond this was a particleboard chicken coop, near-hidden by a field of sodden weeds. Black and white spotted hens crooned and strutted, ruffling feathers. Another dog, a yellow one, led an escape from the fence, through a gap in the makeshift gate. The hound squeezed out next, joining him. They headed for the reeking pond, where they wallowed, legs and tails black and dripping in the muck.

When Ana knocked at the front door there was a long wait, then a heavy scuffling. The latch wriggled and Margaret's whole body appeared, framed by baskets that hung from the ceiling. Today she had two braids, both flipped forward across the broad, generous chest.

"Come in," she said. She didn't smile.

Ana followed her inside, ducking her head as she climbed the narrow, rubber-matted steps. She smelled strong coffee, bacon, a litter box gone too long without cleaning. Cats, one white with a royally plumed tail, a fat, brown tabby, and one scruffy orange, gathered around her. They circled her, rubbing against her legs.

"I was headed out to feed the chickens," Margaret said.

"Need help?" Ana asked. Margaret didn't look like she'd been headed out for anything. Her skin was a grayish-yellow, and she leaned on the counters as she moved from one to another.

"No," Margaret said.

"Are you feeling all right?" Ana asked. She hadn't remembered seeing her like this before. Maybe it was just the dim light, or maybe she had a cold. Something that would clear up when the weather got better.

"Couldn't be better," Margaret said. "I got my coffee, I'm good to go." She tried a weak grin out on Ana, but then let it fall. "Want some?"

"Sure," Ana said. She slipped herself into the narrow space between the kitchenette table and the wall, and sat in a plastic dinette chair. Emmy didn't sit. Instead, she went to work in the little kitchen, building a fort of turned-up chairs. She bumped her head on the bottom of the Formica table, toppled a bowl of sugar. Ana picked it up and brushed the table clean with a dishrag. Margaret clanged around, rummaging through enamel pots and pans, digging spoons and cups out of soapy water. Ana waited, distracting herself with the baskets. The room was overflowing with them. Some were woven with bright feathers, some had shiny jingles that sounded like wind chimes when she passed her fingers through them.

The cats roamed the counters and jumped on and off the table. The brown tabby crouched under a parakeet cage that hung from the ceiling, then flung himself at it. Margaret grabbed a broom and swatted him off, and he lumbered off in indignation. The parakeet ruffled blue feathers, wheezed in terror. Emmy abandoned her fort and made a lunge for the cat, missing him when he darted away. She chased him to a narrow hallway, almost knocking one of the baskets down.

"Careful!" Ana said.

Emmy reached up to catch it in sticky-fingered hands. "Could I make a basket?" she asked.

Ana slipped her fingers across the buckskin fringe of a basket that hung above them.

"Maybe," Margaret said, and handed Ana a cup of coffee. "I sell those at Indian Market," Margaret said. She started to rummage through dusty sacks for chicken feed, scooping cupfuls into an empty coffee can. "The ones I don't sell, I keep."

"They're amazing," Ana said. She wanted to ask what she'd come to ask, but she was nervous. Frank wouldn't like it. He didn't approve of her talking to anyone about anything, much less about their life at home. "Personal," he always said. "Nobody's business." She forced the words out.

"I was wondering if I could borrow your chainsaw." She whispered the next part, trying to keep it from Emmy. "I want to get a Christmas tree. It's a surprise." The orange cat bumped against her, rubbed his face against her hand.

Margaret's eyes narrowed to an obsidian slit, but there was a smile behind them. She nodded, gestured to Ana to follow her, and led her outside to a clearing. Emmy stayed close, holding on to Ana's shirt. Tools lay scattered around a stump, and beside them, a chainsaw—candy apple red. Ana picked it up. It was light, not as heavy as Frank's.

Margaret took it from her, yanked the pull cord. "Start it like this," she said. There was a tremor in her arm as she held the saw, though she pretended it was nothing. "See?" she said, and the engine revved up, like a one-cylinder miracle.

Ana was excited. Frank had never shown her how to do this. It didn't seem so hard. "I'll get it back to you soon," she said.

"No hurry," Margaret said. She moved to the chicken yard, started to scatter feed. The hens scurried as she dipped, tossed, dipped again. She turned and stopped, then turned again. Her braids slipped forward and back as she moved. It might have been a graceful, ceremonial dance, but for an awkward roll of ankle to knee.

Margaret watched Emmy as she followed the chickens. They flapped and pecked at her legs, making her squeal. "Go," Margaret said to her, pointing to the straw in the makeshift henhouse. "Check for eggs." Then she turned to Ana, walked her to the end of the fence, then pointed to a tree that towered over all the others. "See that tall ponderosa?"

Ana nodded.

"There's a trail starting there. At the ridge. It goes out to Holy Ghost Creek. Nobody is ever out there. You'll find what you want out there."

"I'll try that," Ana said. She found herself smiling at Margaret, wondering if there was anything this woman couldn't do on her own, by herself.

"Isn't Daddy getting a tree?" Emmy asked. She'd crept up on them silently and now stood before them, alternating her weight from one foot to the other, holding a brown egg gingerly, in both hands.

"Ana's answer was quick, nervous. "I'm just getting firewood," she said. Margaret raised one eyebrow. Ana avoided her eyes. It was too hard to explain.

"That egg for me?" Margaret said to Emmy, holding out her hands.

Emmy nodded and rolled it into her palms.

"It's going to snow tomorrow," Margaret said.

"I hope," Ana said. "Maybe the road will freeze up."

"With any luck," Margaret said, and turned away.

Ana picked up the chainsaw. "Thanks for everything."

"Any time." Margaret headed back to the motor home, leaving the feed can where she'd put it down. The chickens crowded around it, shoving each other, picking at it until it tipped over and spilled. But Margaret didn't stop to fix it. She disappeared back into the trailer. Ana didn't care what she said-she didn't look well. She pictured her curling back into bed with a ragged wool blanket, sleeping till sundown.

Margaret's orange cat followed her home. She reached down to scratch his neck, and he curled his tail around her hand. She wished "No Cats" wasn't one of the things on Frank's long list of rules. He hated cats. His mother had left him in charge of her cat when she'd run off with the lawyer, he explained. Every time he'd gone to feed it, he told Ana, he'd wanted to strangle it instead. So Ana left the cat, reluctantly, in the cold, and took Emmy inside.

She searched for something to feed Frank for dinner. In the freezer was fish, some ice cubes, a bag of green chile, frozen solid. She reached for the deep fryer at the top of the refrigerator. The plastic lid had slipped off, and there was a thick layer of lard at the bottom, shiny, like pale cadaver skin. The fat heated quickly, popping and sputtering as she set the table. She wondered if there were still some old french fries in it from the week before, and dipped in a slotted metal spoon, searching. Fat spattered onto her arm as she lifted the spoon, and she almost dropped it. Her stomach turned. There, cradled against the dripping slots, was the cooked carcass of a mouse, its gray flesh crisp, still clinging to the bones. It must have climbed in for food, trapped itself there. Ana gave it a hasty burial under one of the cedars, then scrubbed the fryer clean.

She turned the oven on, then hesitated. Frank always wanted his fish to be fried. He said the oven made things taste funny, though she didn't think so. She left the fryer on the counter. She would bake the fish; he didn't need to know. If he asked, she'd say it was fried.

In the end, Frank didn't know what she had done. He only scowled when she mentioned she had to work that night, and the next.

"You have to?"

"Always on Mondays and Tuesdays," she said.

"This fish tastes stale," he said.

"I'm sorry." Ana waited, but he didn't say more.

It seemed like her breath had been stuck in her chest all day, and now it was coming out all at once. She breathed back in, strong and full, so full her lungs felt ready to burst. It felt good, making dinner the way she wanted to. Next she resolved to get wood, to cut her Christmas tree.

An electric heater hummed and rattled from the corner by the piano. After dinner, Frank sat on the floor with Emmy where she was sprawled, stacking dominoes in a long neat row, like the great wall of China.

"More," Emmy said, and he started another row. She waited until there were two long walls, until he nodded, and she pushed at the end, making the first ones topple, then all of them fell, rippling.

"Again," Emmy said, and he started again.

Ana always marveled at his patience with Emmy. He was a different man, sometimes. Not the way he was with her, as a husband.

She leaned over to pick up the wood basket, easily, as if he would-for once-be patient with her.

He stopped stacking the dominoes, shot her a glare. "What are you doing?"

"I'm going to get some wood." She bit her tongue. She didn't say, "because you haven't."

"I told you I'd get it," he said.

"I know. But I have a good place to get it. Don't worry-it's not on our land." She felt her grip tighten on the handle of the basket.

He scowled. "What are you going to cut it with?"

"I borrowed Margaret's chainsaw," she said, and waited for his reaction.

It stunned him a little, she could tell. He hadn't remembered to make a rule against this.

"You don't know how to use it," he said.

"Margaret showed me." Her cheeks were hot, the blood pulsing at her temple. She turned from him so he wouldn't see her, wouldn't hear the angry pounding in her chest. She decided to start moving, to stick to her plan, whatever he said. She carried the basket to the door.

"Go on then," he said. "Do it yourself."

She didn't answer. The last thing she saw before the door slammed shut behind her was Emmy knocking down the stack of dominoes, pulling at Frank for his attention, turning his ever watchful eyes from her, if only long enough for her to get away. She didn't stay to see more. Emmy had saved her, this time, and she was grateful.

She grabbed the chainsaw from under the stairs where she'd stashed it, walked away from the house as fast as she could. She headed for the creek, working her way down the fault of the mountain, climbing over jutting slabs of limestone, rocks that once were coral, rocks with gleaming mica, glittering pyrite. It was dead, she thought, this petrified sea of rock, where warm ocean water had once sheltered life. The trees now had to grow in the spaces between the rocks. They were starved. For water, for earth. For something to let their roots sink into, something to hold on to, so they could live. The branches were dry, cracking as she wove her way through them.

Her lungs filled with the dusty scent of pitch and juniper. The forest was still in the light of the fading sun. There wasn't the usual movement, of cottontails, lizards. Only a thin crust of snow remained on the ground. There was that, at least, she thought. The snow. The sun that melted it. There would be some water, at least. A breeze came up, making the trees groan and scrape. She looked up at the gnarled branch of a cedar, startled by the stare of Margaret's orange cat. He jumped down and followed her.

There was a makeshift footbridge before her, just a few silver-gray logs laid over rocks. The creek ran below, just a trickle of water over a sun-baked *arroyo*. She set foot on the bridge lightly at first, but it was stronger than it looked. She was halfway across when she saw it. It was a sturdy piñon, the Christmas tree she'd been hoping to find. The twisted cedars wouldn't do, and most of the junipers were fat and bunchy. But this tree was broad at the base, tapering raggedly off toward the top. This was as close to perfect as she would find.

She thought of Frank at home, of how he watched her when she was there, her every move. She was sick of it. He wasn't here now, she told herself. There was just silence, broken only by the wind that came through the trees and retreated, like a wave. She thought of Michael, of what he'd said about freedom. She thought of the way he opened the door for her, of the warmth of his hands, his eyes. He made her feel strong, somehow. able to look beyond Frank, beyond the rules. She stepped off the bridge onto solid ground. She picked up the chainsaw, yanked the cord. The cat scrambled away at the sudden roar. The saw whined through the brown, obstinate trunk. Splintering wood followed, a violent cracking, and then the fall. Musty earth gave way to the slap of the tree. She set to work on the firewood, cutting a scrawny juniper overgrown with mistletoe. Sweat froze on the back of her shirt, but she finished, carrying the narrow logs back to the house, stacking them neatly against the back porch. Then she went back for the tree. She dragged it home, up the steep narrow pathway that led to the ridge. Her fingers were numb, her cheeks stinging from the cold. By then, Frank was in one of the back rooms; she could hear him hammering sheetrock.

In a clearing at the back of the house she filled a plastic bucket with water and stones, holding the tree in place. The cat had followed her all the way home. He lapped water from the bucket, his fire-colored fur dusty and ragged. She left him to put a stack of wood inside, then returned with a bowl of milk. He drank it, gratefully. Tomorrow, she decided, she would tell Frank she wanted to keep the cat, if Margaret would let her have it. She didn't care what he said. She would bring it inside, along with the Christmas tree. It would be the only present she would ask for. He couldn't say no.

The next day, when she brought it up, he said what she'd learned to expect. He sat in his La-Z-Boy, cleaning his rifle. He was headed out for target practice. He didn't want to be bothered.

"No way," he said. "Why do you even want that filthy cat?"

"Why does everything always have to be your way?" Ana asked. She felt the rage again. She wanted to grab his rifle, chop it up for firewood, burn it. She hated it.

Frank shook his head. "You're wrong. You're the one trying to get your way. You're always getting us into shit like this."

"Like what?" Ana asked.

"Like trying to tell me to work on that Indian's driveway," he said.

Ana shut her eyes. "Forget it," she said. "Forget I ever mentioned it."

"I ought to shoot those goddam animals up there," he said.

Ana swallowed a bitter laugh. What was the point? She would hold it in. She still had a long day ahead, a long night of work. She turned away, resolving not to try again.

6

At St. Joseph's the wards jangled in a false cheeriness, a nauseating parody of Christmas. The volunteers had gilded the rooms from top to bottom in silver tinsel. In the emergency room, three doctors crowded around one bed, their green scrub suits soaked in a man's bright red blood. There was the smell of something, a stark, gray smell, death. "Another stabbing" was all the information she had from the lab.

In the room next to the dying man was an elderly woman lying on a gurney. When Ana came in, she didn't move. A man was there, her husband, Ana guessed. He held the woman's hand. Their clothes were threadbare, too big for their bodies. Michael found her there as she drew the woman's blood, helped with the needles and tubes. Slowly, Ana realized, under the usual sounds of the ER, the clanking and bumping, the commands of the doctors, there was a foreign sound. It was soft, sweet, plaintive. It was the old man, playing a harmonica. He played as if courting the woman.

Michael took hold of Ana's arm, gently, and she felt his body standing close to hers. "Think she can hear him?" he whispered.

The woman was dreaming, the deep-lidded eyes darting back and forth beneath papery brown skin.

Ana nodded and gathered the tubes. She felt tears welling in her eyes, and she didn't know why. She couldn't recognize the song, but it was one of those old *canciones* she'd heard as she drove by wedding receptions at the rickety, wood-framed dancehall in La Cueva. A love song. One of the stanzas triggered Ana's memory of some of the words. "*Solo Tu*, Only You..."

"Can you meet me at Tino's?" Michael asked.

"Not tonight," she said, but her heart was racing again.

"Soon, then, after Christmas?"

"I'll try," she said. She left him standing in the hallway. She couldn't bear to tell him no, but she didn't know what would happen if she said yes. She washed her hands at the lab, looked out of the window above the sink. It was snowing again. She thought of the trip back to the house, about getting it over with before the road turned to sludge. She had done her part. The old woman would live or not. If she died, her husband would play the harmonica to himself. At some point, Ana knew, she would have to decide. To let this thing with Michael go on, whatever it was, or not. What to do about Frank, about everything. But not now. Now, she needed to think about getting home, getting up the road.

She could see how it would be. Great globs of mud would fill the wheel wells of the Wagon and grip its frame, and the windshield wipers would smear a sad, brown watercolor across the glass. She wouldn't be able to see where she was going. She had to hurry so she'd be able to keep from sliding into the ditch, into the bottomless slag of mud.

The phone was ringing in the lab. She should answer it. It might be new orders, or Michael, asking again if she would see him. She let it ring. She left, telling the techs they would have to pick up the remaining orders. She would decide, tomorrow.

In the end, she'd been wrong about the drive home. The storm never made its way to La Cueva. The road was still solid, a hard-packed crust. She thought this was her moment of grace, that she could collapse into bed, not think about anything, at least for one night. But instead of falling asleep, she went over everything in her mind, obsessing. By now Ana had no more questions to ask of Michael. She already knew what she needed to know. What she didn't know was the answer to the question inside her heart, how to get away. When she fell asleep that night, she dreamed she was at Holy Ghost Creek, with him. He reached to her blindly, across the space between them. He drew her down to him, beneath the ponderosa. She felt the twisted place in her chest unwinding. The heavy feeling slipped from her, like a clot of sodden earth, dissolving into the air. She saw his soft white shirt falling away, the shine on his skin. She held him, felt the warmth and glide of his thighs. There was the smell of crushed juniper berries, the taste of salt and skin. She felt the shield of his hair falling all around her, tangled and brown between her fingers.

◊ ◊ ◊

Two days before Christmas Ana found herself alone, waiting for Frank to get home. He was out with Joe, and she'd just put Emmy to bed. In the living room, the space she'd cleared among Emmy's toys, for the tree Frank had promised, was still empty. Her secret tree was still at the back of the house. She had a thought. She might go to the closet, get his green-leafed shirt, the one from their wedding. It would be right where he always wanted it hung. Third shirt in, top button fastened, right-facing. She might get the scissors and cut it into a hundred strips, and tie them into neat little bows. She could put one on every branch of her Christmas tree. But she didn't.

She distracted herself, checking the wood basket. It was almost empty, and the fire in the wood stove was starting to go out. She threw in a wad of newspaper to catch the flame. It burned blue for a moment, then flickered out. She added twigs from the bottom of the wood basket. The flame took hold again, but it was slow, lethargic. She went back outside for firewood. The orange cat was there again, huddled under the stairs, his breath hard and slow. Snow glinted on the surface of his fur. She hesitated, thinking of Frank, then decided. She held the door open and coaxed the cat inside. He came up the stairs, one paw at a time, watching her steadily. Then he crept behind the woodstove.

She got back to work on the fire, and at last managed to make it blaze. She wrapped herself in the quilt, but shivered for a long time. She got up once or twice to offer the cat some venison, and he came out to take it. Slowly, cautiously, he came to her, curled in her lap, and began to purr.

When she heard Frank driving up the road, she hid the cat in the bathroom and hurried to bed, pulling the covers up and pretending to be asleep. She could see him from the bedroom door, his face red and wet, his fine hair falling across his eyes. He was carrying a huge Christmas tree. It was perfect, a Douglass Fir. They must have had them on sale at the tree lots, since the holidays were almost over. She watched him set up the tree in the living room, stumbling, drunk. She felt a bitter laugh rising in her throat, but she swallowed it before he got to the bedroom. Too little, too late, she thought.

"Ana?" He reached for her shoulder, but she rolled against the wall.

"Don't," she said.

He breathed on the back of her neck, persistently.

"Not tonight," she said. Hot tears gathered and fell. She held herself still, shut her eyes, and willed herself into a deep, cold sleep.

In the morning, she let the cat out before he woke up. She went to the piñon she had dragged to the house, the secret Christmas tree. She cut it all to firewood. It would keep the woodstove going, at least for one more night.

On Christmas day, there was a storm, and Ana heard the tree branches crack. They were already weak from the mistletoe, and the weight of the snow was breaking them. She determined to make it a good day. She opened presents and said her thank-you's. She gave Frank the flannel shirt she'd bought for him, cigars, hard salami, the things she knew he would like. He gave her a new deep fryer and a pair of fur-lined gloves.

There was one small ritual in which they truly came together, the scuffle to make sure everything was in place for Emmy's pleasure, the short walk down the hall with a lighted candle to wake her and let her know that Santa had come. The tree glowed softly with its old-fashioned lights and a few handmade ornaments Ana had dug out of storage. The reindeer and sleigh had finally been put on display, and presents they'd bought on credit were stacked in clouds of angel hair. There was a shiny green bicycle with sturdy training wheels; a book of fairy tales; a child's tape-recorder with big, square buttons; a doll with curly hair, a yellow dress. But Emmy never abandoned Dooby for anything new. The old sock monkey "helped" her open all her presents, had a front row seat in the bicycle basket when she took her first wobbly ride across the living room. Ana and Frank laughed together for a while, as they had in the old days, when the marriage was new and the disappointments hadn't yet settled in.

It might have gone on that way, if Margaret hadn't hobbled to the house later in the day, lugging some old cross-country skis, poles, and a pair of scuffed boots. Frank had gone out to chop wood, and she arrived while he was away. The broad Apache face peered out of the thick scarf Margaret had wrapped around her head, brown and creased at the corners of the lips. Her breathing was labored by the cold, or by the effort of walking.

"Maybe you can use these," she said, handing the skis to Ana. Strange, Ana thought, that she looked so sad, so resigned. Maybe it was just that she knew the trouble she was about to cause. Frank wouldn't like it. Not one bit. He never wanted her to do anything new, especially without his permission. Still, Ana accepted the gift. She put on two pairs of socks to make up for the oversized boots, then tugged clumsily at the bindings.

Margaret showed her the basics, telling her to keep her backside tucked in and her knees bent, to push off with the poles and to point her toes together when she wanted to stop. Ana managed to navigate her way down the driveway, then back again, falling once or twice, but recovering. She pushed one ski forward and let the other follow, in a long, slow sliding that left her with an unfamiliar feeling of pride.

By the time Frank came back, Margaret was gone, and Ana had made her way around the house, twice. She hadn't fallen again.

He dumped the fresh-cut load of wood at the side of the stairs.

"Where'd you get those?"

The snow was coming down again, fast and thick, and Ana wiped a snowflake from her cheek. She raised her eyes to his face.

"Margaret," she said. She knew what he was thinking. But she wasn't going to acknowledge it.

"Since when did you decide you wanted to ski?" he asked. His eyebrows were up again. Like Mussolini, Ana thought. Or Hitler.

"Is there a problem with skiing?"

"Watch your mouth," he said.

She looked straight into his eyes, determined not to back down. She was tired of arguing about what could and couldn't be done, or the right way and the wrong way of doing the few things that were permitted. Everything, it seemed, must be done his way, or there would be consequences. She refused to lower her eyes.

His face turned red. He reached for the handle of the truck door, got in. He slammed the door and backed all the way out of the driveway. Ana knew he would come back. He had nowhere to go. There was always Joe, good for a few hours, a few beers. He would be out for a while, but he would be home before long.

And so it was, a few hours later Frank crept into bed and touched her back softly, as if nothing had happened. No, she thought. Not tonight. She begged off, saying she was tired. She wished she could lie on the air at the opposite edge of the bed. He would not touch her the way he used to, no matter how far he reached, no matter how hard he tried.

In the morning Ana watched him disappear into the forest carrying his Winchester and an ice chest with a sixpack of tallboys. In a short time, she assumed, he'd shoot up the target and kill the beer, and would be quite pleased with himself. He was wearing a plaid flannel shirt, a baseball cap.

It was only fifteen minutes before she heard it, the predictable crack of a gun, echoing across the mountain. And oddly, he came back to the house right away, the outing already at an end. She was in the living room when he opened the door, crossed the kitchen, and started shuffling around. He was making coffee, spilling sugar, rattling cups.

"That was fast," Ana said.

There was no answer, only an uncomfortable silence. She put down the last of the logs she'd been stuffing in the woodstove and walked into the kitchen.

"Did something happen?" she asked.

Frank cast a narrow-eyed glance at her.

"I shot that orange cat," he said. "I thought it was a rabbit."

"Is he dead?" Ana asked, daring Frank to raise his eyes to hers.

"I said I shot it, didn't I?" He wouldn't look at her. He stuffed his hands in his pockets and kept his eyes on the floor. There was only the sound of a spoon stirring coffee, metal scraping porcelain, over and over, making Ana want to scream. A dark, icy coldness seemed to spin out of her.

"Where is he?" she asked, pulling on a sweater, reaching into a pocket for her gloves.

"Up on the ridge," he answered.

She turned away, too angry to speak. She got her coat, pulled gloves from the pockets, put them on slowly, deliberately, one finger at a time. She opened the door, let it slam behind her.

It didn't take long to find the cat. His body was still soft, but no longer warm. She wrapped him in a towel and laid him in one of Frank's old boot boxes. She took a rusty shovel and headed for the creek. She started to dig, and the wind blew hard against her. The frozen ground wouldn't yield at first, but it finally gave way, enough for her to get through the fractured bedrock. She used the shovel to gouge at the rock, and when that didn't work, she took off the gloves and dug with hands and nails, sobbing, until at last there was a shallow hole.

She stared at the ground. The wind hissed and blew up sheets of air like shattered glass, stinging her eyes. She covered the box with dirt and pine needles and knelt there, so long her legs went numb. The shape of her knees molded themselves into the clay and froze their image into it-two small knots of bone-shape in the earth. When the feeling came back to her legs like pinpricks of ice, she straightened them, holding to one of the junipers as she stood. She would have to make the numbness go away. Her legs would have to carry her home. She didn't want to see his face. He wasn't sorry. She would have to be the one to go to Margaret's, to tell her. She would take Emmy with her. It would be good for Emmy to stay with Margaret sometimes. Away from home she could think, could imagine how things would be if she didn't have to go back.

7

$\mathcal{D}$uring the first week of the new year, the hospital was busier than ever. There was a child, Emmy's age. He had been thrown from a truck bed. He was paralyzed now, helpless. It made Ana sick to see him on a respirator, weak, bloated. In the emergency room, a father of six was on a gurney behind the curtain. Broken. A semi had hit his car head-on. The family held each other, cried.

Michael found her at the lab when she'd stopped in to pick up orders.

"Lunch with me tomorrow?" he asked. There was a long silence, while Ana forgot to breathe. She felt herself flush, like a schoolgirl, she thought. She thought of the lab secretary, a woman with frowsy gray hair and glasses, who was standing behind the counter, listening. But that wasn't going to stop her. This was personal, she thought. Nobody's business.

"Sure." She smiled at Michael, in spite of herself, in spite of the secretary.

"Where?" he asked.

"You pick," she said.

"China Dragon?" He sounded suddenly shy, his boldness fading. But his eyes held hers, willing her not to look away.

"That's good," she said. It was perfect, really, a sleepy café, tucked away behind a railroad station, always deserted. No one would ever see them there.

Michael turned away, glancing back at her as if he expected her to call after him, to say she'd changed her mind. Ana could see Louise standing above her, looking down on her, dictating what she should say: *I'm sorry. I just remembered. I can't. I'm married. I'm a mother. I can't.* But Ana, the schoolgirl, only waved at Michael, to reassure him, and her smile turned to a delighted laugh.

"I'll see you tomorrow," she called after him. Then she returned the stern gaze of the lab secretary, at that moment and for the rest of the day. She didn't care. She was tired of the rules. She wanted to be with this kind man who treated her with respect, this man who was not her husband. She didn't care what anyone had to say about it.

At the China Dragon, she wore her blue dress. She'd put on a long woolen coat, to hide it. She'd told Frank she was going to the mall, to look for shoes. He wouldn't have liked it if he'd seen her wearing it. "Too revealing," he'd said last time she wore it, even though what its ballerina neckline revealed was just a bit of shoulder, innocent. She felt beautiful in that dress. Her hair was pulled back in a silver barrette, and she'd glossed her lips, painted her nails. *Jezebel,* her mother's voice rattled in her head. But she still didn't care. She never wanted to end up like her father–alone, defeated.

The café was a two-story stucco on Guadalupe Street, out of place among the flat brown adobes. The staircase led to high, black-lacquered doors. From the landing, Santa Fe sprawled. The air was wet with snowflakes, and she could see her own breath, could feel the cold at her nose and the tips of her fingers. She opened the doors to a steamy dining room. There was the scent of spice. Star anise, peppercorn, clove, fennel. Michael was waiting. She thought of the list of questions she wanted to ask him, but they all seemed trivial. Still, here they were, together. She knew if she didn't make him talk about himself, they would end up talking about her. She didn't want that. Too much that she couldn't say, that she didn't want to talk about.

She walked to the table where he sat, and he got up to pull out her chair. She charted the slope of his hairline, the shape of his forearm. She sat across from him, trying to pretend a calm she didn't feel.

"Tell me about nursing," she said, after they ordered. "How'd you get into that?"

"I wanted to make a difference. Do something that wasn't about war. Something to make me think maybe the world really could be different."

"Any regrets?"

"No. Never." His eyes never left hers, even when the waiter interrupted to take their orders.

She tried to think of something besides the feel of his knees against hers, the way that scarce touch circled through her, like grass fire, out of control. She watched him as he watched her, believing she knew what was in his mind. That he cared for her too, that he forgave her for being so complicated.

"And the pottery?" she asked. "How did you learn that?"

"From a friend," he said.

"She begged for more details, so he talked of bowls, Moroccan, Japanese, African, Korean. He talked of fire, water, color. He drew on the napkins, explaining raku and saggar firing, fettling, pouring, glazing. He made sketches of a teapot he planned to make, of a rounded bowl he'd just finished. And then, he must have slipped.

"Karen used to help-" he said. His eyes shifted away, the minute he said it.

"Who's Karen?" Ana asked. She had a moment of panic. There was someone else he cared about, something she hadn't expected. She saw his face crumple, but only for a second. And then it was normal again, trying to convince her it didn't matter.

"I was engaged once," he said. "I lost her." He was looking away, out the window, at the other diners, anywhere but at Ana.

"What happened?" She wanted to reach over, to touch his hand. But she waited.

"Car accident." The words were blunt objects, words he was not comfortable saying.

"Can you talk about it?"

"I'd rather talk about you," he said.

Ana let herself fall for this, though she knew he was doing the same thing she had done. He was turning everything away from himself, avoiding anything painful. The food arrived, saving her for a few minutes. But by the time the waiter left, she had let go, had started to tell him everything she thought to be important about herself. She talked of life before Frank and Emmy, of her mother, of college, of her father, who had taught her to fish in the Louisiana bayous, his lantern swinging, smelling of kerosene, casting golden light on mossy water. She told how he used to bait hooks for her, telling her not to cry when the fish gasped for air, letting her throw them back in the water, more often than not.

"Once," she said, "when I was six, I rode his shoulders to a juke shack. He whispered, asking if I wanted to go. My mother didn't know. She'd never have let him take me. There was a big shack behind a Mobil gas station. A black woman played the piano, and sang. She wore perfume, like my mom's, Emeraude. Men drank clear stuff out of those old Ball brand jelly jars, and everyone was dripping sweat. So hot outside even the grasshoppers tried to get in the shack, in the shade. I had to slap them off my legs."

As she talked, she realized she wanted to be known. She kept going, laughing, talking, confessing all her secrets in spite of herself-as if the story could make him know her, who she really was.

"They made cracks about us, the 'coon-ass' and his little girl. It scared me, but I loved it. Oh, and my dad drank a Jax beer, and he bought me an Orange Crush. That piano player sang loud, and sad. It hit me, even then, right in the heart. I'd never heard songs like that. It wasn't my mom's Christian music, that bland stuff, like oatmeal."

Michael laughed, nodded. He speared broccoli on his chopstick, made her stop to eat. She obeyed for a minute, then went on.

"My father asked that woman to keep singing. Sing *Summertime*, he said. He put a dollar in her jar. And she did, she sang it like she was doing it just for him."

Ana talked fast, to mask the heat she felt when Michael touched her hand. She told him that when they'd left the bar, her father said she might as well not tell her mother, that she wouldn't want to hear it. And she told about how from that day on, even though she got some odd, squinty-eyed looks from Louise when she did it, she played her father's records, the black 78s, heavy in her hand, the labels showing through the holes in their thin paper covers. *Aristocrat, Bluebird, Trumpet, Victor.* She played them all-Lonnie Johnson, Sonny Boy Williamson, Blind Boy Fuller. She memorized the names and the words of the hard-voiced women, too–Bessie Smith, Ma Rainey, and the sweet one, Billie Holiday. Not in a million years, her mother said, would she understand why her little girl liked that strange, sad music. But it was her secret, and her father's. She never told why.

Ana and Michael finished eating, almonds spilling as they talked, cracking fortune cookies that declared their fates.

"Good fortune awaits you," Ana's said.

Then Michael read his: "You will soon be honored by someone you respect." The waiter swept them out at closing time, pulling the black doors shut and locking them with what seemed like a vengeance.

They walked down the railroad tracks to get to their cars, still laughing and talking, heads low and close together. There would be more times like this, Ana thought, on the long drive home. Time to let him talk about himself. Time to talk of the things that neither could bring themselves to speak of, yet.

When she stepped into the living room at home, the phone rang, and Frank reached for the receiver. He held it to his ear, briefly, then let it fall.

"They hung up," he said, disgusted.

She left her coat on, stuffed her hands in her pockets, avoided his stare.

"It seems pretty strange, we keep getting all these hang-ups." He turned to the kitchen and started to rummage through the refrigerator.

"It's just somebody with the wrong number," she said.

He mumbled something she couldn't hear.

"Did you say something?" she said. She felt herself trembling, feeling guilty, afraid.

"No," he said.

She went to the bathroom, closed the door, pulled the blue dress off and stuffed it inside the coat, yanked on jeans and a t-shirt. She flushed the toilet, ran the water in the sink.

"What took you so long at the mall?" Frank asked. He was just outside the door.

"They didn't have my size shoe," she said. She came out, put the coat in the closet, crossed to the kitchen. There were dishes on the counter and silverware in the sink. She ran the water, put in soap. Frank had followed. She didn't want to look at him.

His old glare was on her, full force. "What's your problem?" he said.

"Nothing." Sweat gathered on her forehead, her palms.

"I said, what's your problem?" he repeated.

She moved to the table, carrying spoons, forks, knives. He was following her now. She felt something like hysteria rising, and swallowed it. It would do no good to keep arguing. She should ignore him, finish cleaning the kitchen, go to bed.

"Well?" He stood over her, waiting.

"I don't know," she said. Her hands were shaking now. She did know. She was shocked at the thought that came to her, about how good it would feel to jab the fork she was holding right into one of his eyes. They bulged, accusing her. They always accused her, whether she did anything or not. She thought about going to the bedroom and locking the door. But he would follow her. It made her want to scream.

She saw Emmy coming, the top of her head emerging first from the darkened hall. A white gown flapped around her, ghostlike in the dull glow of the kitchen light. She curled her fingers into little fists, rubbing the sleep from her eyes. "You woke me up."

Frank went silent, moved to his La-Z-Boy, sat down. But Ana could still see him tensing, ready to spring.

"I'm sorry, Emmy," Ana said. She felt the fork in her hand, her own throat working itself. The anger still bubbled its way up. "Go back to bed. I'll be there in a minute."

"I want to be with you." Emmy's eyes were wide, pleading.

"Not now," Ana said. She looked at Frank's hands, straining themselves against the hide of the chair.

Emmy tugged at her waist, and she relented. She put down the fork, got up from the kitchen chair, lifted her. She sat on the piano bench, holding Emmy close on her lap. "I'll play one song for you. Then you have to go back to bed."

Emmy's lower lip pushed out, but she nodded.

Ana's fingers moved on the keys, slowly. She played that same old song-*Summertime*. She felt as if she were under water, as if she could barely hear. The notes were slow, deep. She must have been playing an octave too low. All her concentration went into remembering. Which fingers, which keys. She played it like a dirge.

"Ana," Frank said.

Emmy leaned into her, silent, craning her neck to look at him. Ana kept her eyes on the keys, felt her own body going tight. She stopped playing. There was the feeling of Frank's stare, his eyes on the back of her neck. She could picture him, only the muscles moving in his hands.

"You're not going to play?" He rose from the chair and came to lean over her, threatening.

Emmy started to whimper. Ana shook her head. I can't play, I can't, she thought. But the words didn't come out. She held to Emmy as if her life depended on it.

Emmy pulled away from Ana, from both of them, shaking her head, confused. Her chest heaved in angry, animal sobs, and Frank's face contorted. Ana watched him, his attention turning from Emmy back to her.

He stood above her, and his fist swung up and came down. Ana lunged away. The fist swung back and then he hit the wall above the piano. The fine white dust of the bare sheetrock lingered in the air.

His face was red, twisted. "What is the matter with you?"

"Nothing," she said, almost whispering, her spine curved, chin down, submissive. Tears gathered at the corners of her eyes, slid down. She was afraid to move, afraid to lift her hand to wipe them away. "Nothing."

He turned and left the house, slamming the door behind him.

Ana forced herself to focus on the blur her child's face had become, reaching for her. Emmy flinched but allowed herself to be drawn up. She was crying, her face covered with hectic red blotches. Ana made her blow her nose, then tucked the quilt around her and rocked her to sleep. She felt a cold depression creep in. She was crazy to think Frank would ever change. And even if she thought of escaping him, he would never let her go. Not without a fight like this, or something worse.

$\mathcal{T}$he next time Ana wore the blue dress, it was for a party. Frank's boss expected them to attend, and there was no getting out of it. Frank made it clear that he disapproved of her choice the minute she put it on. His eyes settled on the ballerina neckline, on the curve of her shoulders.

"I wouldn't have thought of that one." It sounded sarcastic. This was not the way Michael had looked at her, had spoken to her. Michael had made her feel beautiful, smiling to see her in something other than the old lab coat.

"I'll wear the white one," she said. She didn't want to make trouble. It was the only other good dress she had, white wool, long sleeved.

"Suit yourself," he said. He searched the closet, slapping hangers together, frustrated. "Have you seen my green shirt?" he asked. He was angry.

"It's in there," she said. He could find it himself. She reached back to unzip the dress, slipping it off, pulling on the white one. She should have cut that shirt to pieces, she thought, that horrible wedding shirt.

At the party, the house was overheated, and Ana was insufferably hot. She stood in the doorway, trying to cool off. She watched Emmy run with the other children, in and out of the house, laughing, falling down in the dry grass. She tried to shake off her anger, but couldn't.

"What's wrong?" Frank asked. Joe was with him, and they both reeked of beer. They were unshaven, unsightly. She was ashamed to be seen with them.

"It's too hot in here," she said.

Frank studied her, she supposed, to satisfy himself that she would endure the rest of the afternoon. "We won't stay long," he said. "Just long enough to eat," he added. It was for Joe's benefit, but Joe didn't hear him. He had already stumbled away, toward the cooler, looking for beer.

Ana stayed inside to avoid them, though she thought she would faint from the heat. She sipped cheap wine from a plastic cup, studying the rectangles of white light that fell from plate-glass windows across a rug with an Arabian design. There were gold and black patterns in it, something too methodical in it, as if it had been woven according to orders. She imagined a sheik, and a slave woman weaving. She willed herself to smile, to speak politely to the other women there, wives, mostly. But she could hardly bear it. She was no longer able to pretend that nothing was wrong.

At home, she ran a deep bath, pouring rosemary oil into the torrent of water from the faucet. A mist of steam lifted, smelling of green. She heard Emmy cry, a tired-child cry, not one of pain, she decided. Frank would have to take care of it. She sank into the tub, letting her hair float on the surface of the water, like seaweed. Emmy's cry persisted, and she was vaguely aware of it. But there was only one thing on her mind. She was thinking of when she would be with Michael again. She was safe with Michael. She could breathe when she was with him. And she wanted to see him alone, again.

In the morning Ana took Emmy and walked up to Margaret's, offering to help her find the sumac she needed for her baskets-wanting just to be away from Frank. Margaret was only too happy to accept. She seemed tired, as usual, but she insisted on driving. "We'll need the truck to haul everything in," she explained. She wheeled the Toyota deftly around the boulders and through the dip, not even pausing when Henry stepped into the road in front of the gate, folding his arms. The rottweillers, hackles bristling, raced at the truck, but Margaret went on, skidding past at breakneck speed. She seemed to take stock of Henry and find him lacking, the angry brillo hair, the sun glinting off his glasses. In the side mirror, Ana could see his head bobbing, then finally disappearing from view. She laughed to realize he had no effect on Margaret whatsoever. This was a lesson, she thought, and took note of it. He could do, say, whatever he wanted-Margaret would never shut the gate.

At the river they pulled Emmy down the rocky path in a rusted Radio Flyer Wagon, Emmy clutching Dooby, and the wagon wobbled crazily over every bump. The river smelled of grass turned to straw, of small muddy stones. The day was cold but dry. The last of the seed-pods hung from the elms, dry as parchment, rattling in the wind. Margaret sat to rest on a flat shelf of rock.

Emmy flopped onto her broad lap, throwing her arms backward.

"I'm hungry," she groaned dramatically.

Margaret reached into a pocket and found piñon nuts. She cracked one of the small brown shells between her teeth. "Open," she said, holding the nut to Emmy's mouth.

Emmy's eyes widened with suspicion, but she took it on her tongue, chewed it, then opened her mouth for another. Margaret grinned. "Piñons will make you strong," Margaret said. "You should eat lots of them."

"Why?" Emmy said.

"So you can be strong. Save the world, like Changing Woman."

"Who's that?" Emmy said.

Margaret reached for a handful of clay from the river's edge. She squeezed it and rolled it and shaped a round, fat woman, and put it in Emmy's hands. "It's our tradition," she said. "Apaches believe this, that when a girl becomes Changing Woman–" She said it slowly, as if choosing her words carefully. "–her family has to be there to help mold her, like clay, into the right shape. So she can grow up strong and hard."

"Why?" Emmy asked. She studied the clay woman, holding it tenderly.

"That's how she needs to be, to keep the world going," Margaret said.

Ana studied her face, seeing that there was some secret there, that she wasn't ready to let go. Whatever it was had made her ready to crumble inside, back to the river, dissolving out of the woman she was.

"It was in Ruidoso, where I had my ceremony," Margaret added. When I was just a girl." She shifted her body on the rock, moving as if it pained her, then went on.

"There were shelters of pine and oak, with leaves for shade. Wickiups, we called them. At night, we slept in them, to get ready. In the morning, there was wood smoke in our noses, we could hear the drums. It had rained, and the elms were wet. There were birds everywhere. The women were cooking, like always. Fry bread, mutton, posole. I couldn't wait to eat, but Grandmother told me I had to. I had to stay and watch while the men put up the teepee."

Margaret used her hands for the next part, and they waved and stretched, making Ana think of the birds in the elms.

"They stretched a big white canvas tight over poles," Margaret said. "The poles stuck out at the top, twisted, into the sky. They packed the earth around it, in a circle. They took off their hats with the feathers and long leather straps, wiped their faces. When it was time, I was the first one to go in. I was humble, like Grandmother told me. I went to the circle, holding my hands together. I had my buckskins on, and the cattail drinking tube to keep my lips from touching water. Those were the rules. I didn't mind. It was an honor. There was a white feather at the back of my head. That was a prayer, that I would live to the age of white hair. I had an abalone shell, here." She touched her forehead, and a fit of coughing took over.

Emmy wriggled in impatience, and Margaret gave her a slit-eyed glance.

"You all right?" Ana asked.

"Sure," Margaret said. She made the coughing stop, and went on. "Changing Woman hid from a flood, inside an abalone shell. That's how she started everything over again, when the world was ruined."

Emmy reached for another nut, tried to crack the shell herself. It splintered and she spit it out, tried a new one.

"The ceremony," Margaret said, "was for health, for happiness. Long life, strength. My helper showed me how to move my feet, to make the steps. She had me pound a cane on the ground, beating it in time to the drums. When I danced, my dress danced with me, all the jingles clinking, and I prayed, like they told me. Grandmother and Uncle, everybody prayed for me. I danced and danced, with the others dancing behind me, all night long."

For just a moment, Margaret sounded happy. But her eyes went dark again. Ana could see pain, not just the physical pain that always seemed to be with her, but something else. Margaret must have stuffed it somewhere, managed to ignore it, for a very long time. There had always been something behind those eyes, Ana thought, the lips that had to try so hard, just to smile.

"It had all been set," Margaret said. "I would have power. I would be strong and hard, beautiful. That was how it should have been."

"I wanna be Changing Woman," Emmy said. She had mastered the art of piñon cracking, was lining the nutmeats up along the flat of Margaret's palm.

"You've got a long wait," Margaret said. "But when you're old enough, it will happen."

"What do I have to do?" Emmy asked. "To make it soon."

"You can start by cutting the sumac for me," Margaret said. "I'm too tired to do it myself."

So Emmy helped Ana while Margaret told them what to do. They found the sumac and cut it, bundled it together. By the time they had finished and trundled themselves back to Margaret's truck, it was nearly sunset. They piled their treasures in first-Dooby, the sumac, and a hunk of clay Emmy said she was going to use, to make a mud woman all her own.

On the long ride home, Emmy fell asleep, her head hanging forward, resting on Dooby's soft brown body.

"There's something I have to tell you," Ana said. She was counting on the fact that Margaret was driving, would have to keep her eyes on the road. She didn't want to face her when she made this confession.

"What," Margaret said. She looked at Ana anyway, her hands holding the wheel steady, the highway clear ahead.

Ana swallowed, a bitter taste in her mouth from what she had to say. "Frank shot that orange cat of yours."

Margaret looked at the road again. "On purpose?"

"I don't think so," Ana said. "But you never know."

Margaret lifted a hand from the steering wheel, rubbed her nose as if smelling something bad. "You should leave him," she said. He isn't good for you."

"I can't," Ana said.

"Why not?" Margaret still looked sour, waiting for an explanation.

"I'm afraid of him." Ana wondered if Margaret would turn her face to see her, to see the truth of it.

"Why?" Margaret asked. She turned for just a moment, but Ana saw Emmy from the rearview mirror then, shifting in her car seat, opening groggy eyes. She locked her gaze on Ana, watching, listening.

"Shh," Ana said to Margaret. "Not now. Later."

Emmy squirmed, and Ana realized she had been saved from Margaret's scrutiny. She didn't want to talk about it, didn't even want to think about what she had just said out loud, for the very first time. Yes, she was afraid of Frank. Too afraid to speak of it, yet she knew she must deal with it. She had to escape, to find a way out.

At home, the house was chilly, and Frank wasn't home. Ana built a fire in the woodstove, stacking twigs, then branches and logs. She stoked the fire to a roaring blaze and went to get ready for bed. In one of the bureau drawers, she spotted a notebook. She picked it up and flipped through it, reading old notes Frank had written about her when they were dating. She turned one page, and it all came back to her.

"*The rules,*" it said at the top, then:

1) Family first.
2) No friends.
3) Follow new rules, when I come up with them.

He'd used a felt-tip pen to record his conditions. She'd read them before, but that was before they were married, and she hadn't taken them seriously. What struck her now was the self-righteous belief that he could force his will on her. It was the way he always talked to her. Part of it made sense. Louise had always said Ana was just like her father. That she was so bad, she needed someone like Frank to keep her in line. But maybe Louise had been wrong. Maybe Frank was wrong. Maybe she was a good person, just as she was, despite what she had been led to believe. Surely she was not so bad that Frank was all she deserved. What had she been thinking when she married him? She understood now, what she needed in her life was that *shibui* Michael had spoken of-some room, some freedom. She watched the lively, yellow fire as it crackled in the woodstove. Just before she left for work, she ripped the notebook pages out and burned them, one by one.

9

The next day at work Ana picked up Michael's message on the lab phone.

"Are you ready for lessons?" it said.

She laughed and called him back. "Lessons for what?"

"Pottery. Like we talked about. Tomorrow's my last day off for a while. And I know you're off too. I can teach you if you want."

"I thought you wanted to go to Tino's." She was stalling, wanting to go, but still afraid.

"I do, but you said you wanted to learn. This is your chance."

He was waiting for an answer. It was tempting. There would be time, precious time to spend with him without the fear of getting home late. She could lie, tell Frank she had to work.

"Yes," she said. "Yes." And when she left home the following day, she put on her lab coat as usual, as if she was going to work. She said goodbye to Frank, to Emmy, and met Michael on the outskirts of town, following his Trailblazer up a washboard road, almost dry after the recent snow. When they took the final bend in the road, an adobe house came into view, smooth and rounded, like a mud dauber's nest. Cottonwoods stood in the leaves they'd shed, and the sun was full and warm.

"I have some things to fire," Michael said, leading her to a room with a pine-framed workbench. There was a riot of half-used paint jars, finished and unfinished pots, dusty crocks of glaze, chunks of clay in smeared plastic bags. The room smelled of mud and water. He loaded unfired pots into flat cardboard boxes lined with shredded newspaper. He was quiet, deliberate, his hair falling long and wild around his shoulders. Ana watched him without self-consciousness, intently, hungrily, her eyes following every step he took. She ran her fingers across the well-worn surface of the bench, then pressed her palms flat against the wood. There was something about it; it made something shake loose in her body. Her arms and legs suddenly felt weak, unbolstered.

He mixed clay with scraps from a bucket and broke it down, the wet sound slapping against his hands, palm to palm, massaging it like a fat healthy baby, like a well-kneaded bread. When he pushed against it, she watched it yielding, ready to be shaped. His hands were steady and sure, and he seemed to know what the result of every movement would be. The motor of the wheel hummed against the silence. There was no hesitation. He clapped the clay to the center of the stone. Then he opened it, and a pot was born.

His fingers met around the circle of the base, pulling the walls out and up, shaping it. When the pot took its final form, it was beautiful-sturdy and tall, a glittered brown. It was magic, his gathering up of the useless, turning it to gold. Ana watched as he worked and explained. She believed him when he said her hands would learn to listen to the clay, to hear the right way to pull a strong base up into tall slim walls.

Late in the day she followed him outside to the kiln shed, a shack with a roof of tin and fiberglass. Fuel for the kiln-piñon and juniper-was jammed into a smaller shed nearby. The kiln door opened to a dusky interior. She peered in, running her hand along the rough brick surface of the walls.

Michael let his hands brush hers as he showed her how to stack the pots in the kiln, leaning them against each other. He knelt to arrange the wood, and lit the fire with a long match. He stoked the flames until the draft was high, and she watched him move through his work, the long laces of his boots bound around his jeans, the lean, corded muscles, sweat-drenched and silhouetted by the light of the kiln's loading port. The pots glowed like spectral eggs, in currents of white-orange heat. A storm started to come in, clouds rolling overhead. When sleet started to clatter on the roof Ana followed him back to the house, leaving the fire to burn itself out.

In the kitchen she stood at the sink, her hands smudged with oil-black soot. She ran water over them, dried them absent-mindedly, and brushed bits of ash and wood from the tangle of her hair. She could feel him standing behind her, watching her, and she felt the blood rise in her face. He put his hands on her waist and leaned into her. She felt his face on her neck, and the unraveling began.

"I can't." It was what she wanted, what she'd dreamed of, planned for. And yet she wasn't ready. It wasn't possible. It was too dangerous.

"You can," he whispered.

"I shouldn't have come." She held to the porcelain of the sink, as if it could save her. His hands touched her neck, her shoulders.

"It's too complicated." She could barely hear herself. Maybe she hadn't said it at all. Maybe she didn't want to say it. But she had said it. She knew when he answered her.

"Shhh," he said. His hands ran like water down her arms, his fingers encircling hers. He turned her to him and kissed her, and it was deep and sweet, a kiss that said everything he had said to her with his eyes, and more. He pulled at her gently, and she at him, and the clothes were then everywhere, his warm, chapped hands on her skin, and there was no turning back, just the moving, arching, moving through the kitchen to his bed, and the taste of his salt was in her mouth, and the wet of the rain, and he slid into her, like a hand opening clay, firm, sure, shaping. Her hands explored him, roaming. His hair was unbound, falling against her shoulders. She let her eyes close, felt him inside her. She couldn't stop what was about to happen. Heat, sparks, gathered and entered her like wood flame. He stoked the fire, and everything gathered together and burst out, sharp colors turning to white light, searing, melting all that was in her to a tender, gentle form, clear as glass, heavy as gold. It was alchemy, the fire dancing in white-orange heat, purging, melding, making her want to weep. He stilled his body and let her move against him, breathing, her voice escaping, the air in the room and inside her body hot, exploding, breaking, running, earth turned to fire.

This was what she wanted. This man loved her, irrationally. She could tell it in the way he traced her face, the way he captured her hand and held it, pretending she would not have to leave him. And she felt that she loved him, too. She wanted to know everything he knew, everything he was. She wanted to know how to make a glaze of robin's egg blue, the way to shape a pot just so, with a solid base and a sweet-sloping rim. She wanted to learn the right moment to take red-hot pots from the kiln, how to quench their heat. Most of all, she wanted to learn a way to be with him, her fingers brown with slip, pushing into the clay. She would see him again. She deserved this time, this feeling of love. She was tired. Lonely. She saw suddenly and clearly, the silence of her life with Frank, the way she had stifled her own heart, wanting to protect herself but failing miserably.

Instead of the freedom her father had tried to show her, the deep, gutteral music, she'd settled for the measured, restrained stanzas of her mother. She had traded one restricted life for another, without ever asking herself what she really wanted. Here while Michael held his arm around her, like the cusp of a moon, the sadness slipped away. She wanted to stay with him forever.

At home, when she walked into the bedroom, Frank was asleep. She stood at the dusky mirror in the bathroom, studying her own face, the dark eyes that had always seemed brooding before, now lit with a blazing fire. Her lips were swollen, still bruised and tender. She peeled off the shirt and jeans she'd put back on only an hour before. Tomorrow she'd wash them. Tomorrow she'd find Michael, again. Frank would punish her if he found out, would kill her or Michael, or what else God only knew. But this wouldn't stop her from going again. All the twisted places inside her had come unwound.

10

*T*he road, when the last of the snow dried up, was dry and rocky. It had to be navigated methodically, Ana taking one wheel at a time over the boulders, to keep from ripping off the muffler. When she finally came to the end of the road, she got out to open the gate. She didn't intend to shut it. She was headed for Michael's house. She had gone there again and again over the past month, and this time would be no different.

Henry was home, stepping out to block her.

"Are you shutting the gate?" he shouted.

"No!" Ana shouted too. She was tired. She didn't care.

"Stupid bitch!" He moved to her window so fast it frightened her.

"I told you. Shut the fucking gate." He leaned inside, and she could feel his breath on her cheek, sour, reeking of beer.

She turned her face away from him toward the highway, took her foot off the brake, hit the gas.

He jerked his hands back as the Wagon jolted away.

No more would he tell her what to do, she thought. She wouldn't shut the gate. She'd run over him if she had to, if he bothered her again. No one was going to tell her what to do, how to live. And that included Frank.

Lately, so she could see Michael, she lied whenever she thought she could get away with it. She became adept at it. She made up stories-that she had to get groceries, or that her mother was sick-that she had to go to

Albuquerque, knowing full well that Louise was out of town, that she wouldn't be there if Frank called to check on her. She gambled on it. She had a backup plan, in case he ever checked on it. She wouldn't offer any information, and if he said anything, she'd explain that the car had broken down, that she'd never arrived, that her mother wouldn't have known where she was when he called because she'd never made it there. The Wagon *had* broken down, many times, leaving her stranded on the highway. When Frank first bought it, it was a good car. But after a few months on the road, the shocks gave out and the brakes failed. Then the muffler got dislodged and started scraping against the boulders. When the alternator went out Frank managed to get it going again, but then the battery died. It was always something. And when it broke down completely, his orders to Ana were to pull it over to the side of the highway, to wait for him to rescue her.

One night this happened, and she had lain in the back seat for over two hours, her coat tucked around her, shivering but as still as possible, so no one could see her. She told herself that only one woman had ever been murdered on the highway, and that was at the crossing farther up, toward Cañonicito.

That woman had stopped, dutifully, at the stop sign by the church. The man had run up from nowhere, reaching into her open window, demanding the keys to her truck. She made her arguments, in retrospect, hopelessly, since she was about to be murdered. She struggled enough to scrape his skin beneath her fingernails, just enough for the coroner to find later. He'd shot her in the head, just above the ear where her dark hair had been slicked back in a ponytail. Then he had shoved her onto the floor of the truck and covered her with a tarp she'd just bought at the builder's supply. He had driven her to Alabama, then botched an attempt to burn her body in heap of garbage.

Ana reminded herself that the Wagon was so ugly no one would want to steal it. And there was no way it would ever hold up all the way to Alabama. She laughed at herself. She was done with following Frank's rules. His rules would be the end of her. She told him that errands had to be run, or she waited until she knew Frank would be away with Joe, or at work. She told him that Margaret would take care of Emmy, for just a little while.

She was obsessed. She loved going to see Michael, loved the thought of his hands on her body, of how they moved something inside her each time she saw them center the clay, or press it just so to a tender lip or gentle curve. She didn't feel judged when she was with him, even when a pot she was turning collapsed, or when she had to leave him, knowing she was going home, to her other life. He went on teaching her, first to form the pots, then the glazing. He taught her to make them by hand, mixing the clay, kneading, wedging, molding. He was patient as he showed her what to do. Saturday after Saturday she learned. When she worried about Frank, about how he frightened her, she pushed the thoughts away.

One of those days, when Frank had to be at work, Ana took Emmy to stay at Margaret's. She explained-though Emmy stuck out her lower lip as far as it would go-that it was just for a little while, so she could get groceries. She promised Margaret would let her feed the chickens. Even show her how to make a basket. But Emmy latched herself to Ana's leg, wouldn't let go.

"She's scary," Emmy said. "And she's too tired."

"No she isn't," Ana said. She was worried about that too. She didn't know what she was going to do if Margaret didn't start to get better. When they got to her place, the first thing they saw was Margaret holding a bandana to her mouth, stifling a cough.

"What's wrong?" Ana asked.

"It's just old age." Margaret sloughed the question off, scowling at her for asking.

"You should see the doctor."

"Charlatans," Margaret said.

"Charlie-tons?" Emmy asked, still clinging to Ana.

"Quacks," Margaret said, peeling her off Ana, folding her into her own fleshy arms.

"You stay with us," Emmy said, still leaning to Ana, reaching.

"I can't, honey. You need to stay with Margaret."

"Why?" Fat tears waited at the corners of Emmy's eyes, brimming. "Why can't you stay?"

"I just can't. Anyway, it's just for a little while," Ana said. "You want to make a basket, don't you?"

Emmy began to whimper then, and the tears boiled over. She would be all right, Ana rationalized, though Emmy was still pouting when she turned to walk away. Frank wouldn't know the difference. Besides, it would do Margaret good to have some company.

When Ana came to Michael's door, he pulled her to him, closing her mouth with kisses so she could hardly breathe. She felt his heart against hers, hot, wildly beating. There was nothing, nothing she could imagine wanting more. He was the one who left her flowers, blue flax and cosmos, at the nurse's station, in the laboratory. He was the one who met her in the stairwell, stealing kisses, telling her of his love. He was the one to leave secret notes, taped to the inside of her locker door. She didn't care about the price she was paying, about the time lost with Emmy. And some days she hardly thought of Frank at all. She thought he might catch them red-handed, might threaten to kill both of them. But for at least a few hours each week Frank didn't matter, didn't exist.

The next day, she left Emmy with Margaret and went to the grocery store. When she got back, the kitchenette was a riot of branches stripped and coiled. Their clean, woody scent mingled with the dust of feathers, roots and leaves. Emmy pulled branches from soaking water in buckets, stripping the bark with her teeth, like Margaret had taught her.

"Got your groceries?" Margaret asked.

It sounded sly. Ana saw the slant-eyed glances she got whenever she came for Emmy, wondered if Margaret had suspected the truth, about the times she had spent with Michael.

"Did you get the dish soap I asked for?" Margaret stood, stretched out her back.

"I did get you some, but I left it at the house." Ana said. "I'll go back and get it."

"I'll walk with you."

"You don't have to." She was afraid of being alone with Margaret, afraid of confessing all she was hiding.

"I want to. I've been hunched over these buckets all day."

Maybe it was this way of Margaret's, her patience beyond all reason, that made Ana want to confide in her. But still, she kept quiet. Emmy was with them, after all. It wasn't the time for confessions. She led the way, Margaret lagging behind, holding Emmy's hand.

The dish soap was next to Frank's new cigarette lighter in the bags left unpacked on the counter. After they got it, Emmy lured them back outside to the clearing, to her frayed rope-swing, and insisted they stay. Ana pushed her in the swing, watching her stretch spindly legs out against the rushing air, watching Margaret who caught her feet and pushed back.

Ana was distracted, still wanting to talk, to tell someone, anyone, but especially Margaret. "What do you believe in?" she asked. She shut her eyes when she said it, drawing in the dry air, pungent with the smell of cedar, of melting sap. "Sometimes I don't know what I believe in."

"You believe in being a good mother," Margaret said. She leaned back the way Ana had seen her do so often lately, reaching her hand back, resting it at the base of her spine. Margaret seemed older every time she saw her, the fat rope of hair more peppered with silvery gray.

Ana caught Emmy before letting her go again, swinging her high, the way she liked it. "That's true," she said. "I try to be a good mother." But there was another thing. "Honesty," she said. "I believe in honesty. "She studied Margaret's eyes, the darkness there. "I wonder," she said, "what it would really be like to always tell people the truth, whether they wanted to hear it or not." She tried not to feel like a hypocrite. She didn't feel like a good mother. Or a good friend. Or even a good person. Still, she made excuses for herself. All her life she'd had to lie to be accepted. To her mother, to the Sunday School teachers who made her promise to follow the rules, and now to Frank, who had all those rules of his own. The truth was something people didn't want to hear.

There was a sad look on Margaret's face, tender, sympathetic. "Grandmother said if you know the truth, you should say it."

Ana studied her face to see if it was safe to say what she wanted to. The eyes were slitted against the sunlight, but glittering like marcasite. They were centered on her, waiting. It seemed safe to go on, to say more.

"I had a dream the other night," she said. "I was at my mother's, and there was a nest. A bird with her eggs. The bird didn't know it was trapped. I didn't want it to die, so I opened a window. But I realized there was a dog in the house, and when I found the bird again, it was in the dog's mouth. I couldn't do anything."

Margaret's face told it all. "You are the bird," she said. The black eyes snapped then, bright against the sun. "You're going to have to fly."

"I know," Ana said. But she could hear her own voice, timid and quiet, curled far back into her throat, her chest. She was grateful for the silence that followed. There was no more talk of the dream, but she felt she'd started a great confession. There would be time to finish it, later, when Emmy wasn't around. Now, there was only the soft sound of the swing pushing air, of Emmy's protests when Ana said it was time to go inside.

She watched Margaret walking home, envying her noisy, smelly, crazy life alone with her animals and baskets. Emmy pulled at her, wanting her attention. Nothing could be stronger than her love for Emmy, she thought. Not even her feelings for Michael. But there was something stronger, she knew, and that was her fear of Frank.

The first threats had come when she'd told him she was leaving, when Emmy was only six months old. She had already learned, by then, to fear him. He had leaned over her when he said it, his fist in her face. "Try it," he said, and she had dropped it, had given in. There was no winning with him. She might support herself and Emmy, it was true. But he would not let her leave him, so it was pointless to try. He would beat her down at every turn.

◊ ◊ ◊

It rained often at the end of February. The road turned to bog at the bottom of the second hill, where there was still no culvert. Frank never borrowed Joe's backhoe, as he said he would. Ana decided to fix it herself.

She parked on a slab of boulder and climbed out. She wallowed up to her knees in mud, shoveling, pulling logs and rocks over every watery rut, trying to form a crude bridge, a small stretch of dry space. She was angry. It wasn't a road. It was a joke. Nothing but a sinkhole. She should have objected when they bought the land, or at least insisted that everything be finished before they moved in. The line for electricity, running water, the road. She worked until sundown, alone, grateful that no one drove by to see her, ridiculous, her arms and legs awash in red-brown clay. Everything under her collapsed, folded, buckled. She dragged one foot after another, the shoes pulling off, filled with clay. All the softness, deadly, worse than the hard-packed clay and the petrified ruts when the sun was out. She was sick with despair. She imagined it pulling her all the way down, burying her alive, the soft, musty brown filling her nose and mouth, smothering her.

As the last of daylight faded away, she stood in the middle of the road, her hands cut, sore, crusted. It was quiet but for an occasional birdcall. The sun dipped lower and a sliver of orange crowned the mountains. Every time she got one log hauled into place, the slime oozed over it and she had to find another. Her shoulders ached as she hauled in the last of the logs. It was gray, faded, a long-dead juniper. She tried to line it up with where she thought the others must be. Even this sank. A bubble formed in the mud above it and popped, a satisfied, brown belch.

In the Wagon, the heater now malfunctioning and permanently on, blasted her wet clothes like a steam iron. She set her jaw and hit the gas. She would get home and wash up before anyone saw what she'd been trying to do. Frank would say she should have waited for him to get the backhoe. Margaret would say she should make the neighbors pitch in to get the road done right. Henry would say she was a crazy bitch, making trouble again. No one would understand.

11

The workroom was filled with the pottery Ana and Michael had made. The bowls and cups sprouted on his open shelves like unmatched flowers–cobalt blue, gold-flecked yellow, lavender, green. He had been working on a set of mugs, different from the ones he usually did. These were soft-thrown, with orange and black tigers painted on the sides, chasing each others' tails. Ana mixed the final glaze in a jelly jar, and four small pots of color, each with its brush. Black, yellow, orange, red. The room smelled of limestone, salt, oil of turpentine.

"What was it like with her, the girl you were going to marry?" she asked. She wanted reassurance, wanted to know how she measured up.

"It was good," he said. "We knew everything about each other." He painted in delicate strokes with the brush, turning the mug, concentrating.

"Not like us," Ana said. Her own project lay untouched on the bench, a lumpy bowl she'd scrapped three times, given up on.

"No, not like us," he said. His voice was suddenly quiet, distant.

"Will we ever be that way?" she asked. She wondered why she asked it of him, and not herself. She was the one who had the answer. He was the one who was waiting.

"He sighed and put down the brush, closed his eyes as if he was tired. "Not while you're with Frank."

"I'm sorry." She picked up the bowl, turned it, felt the weight of it in her hands. It was a lost cause, irreparable.

"Don't be sorry. Just leave him." He touched her shoulder then, tentatively. "Come live with me."

Ana tried to speak, could not form the words. He gave her plenty of time to think. There was a long, stark silence as he dried his hands, put the brushes in a glass of water, capped the jars of paint, waited.

"You have to get out of it," he said, finally, watching her as she put the bowl down, started to cap the pots and put them away. "This–seeing each other like this–it isn't enough. Not for me, anyway."

"I can't. He won't let Emmy go."

"You'd get custody. There's nothing he could do."

"I don't know." She could tell he wondered why she was afraid. "He scares me."

"Why? Has he hurt you?"

Her cheeks burned with shame, giving her away. "I think he would, if he knew about us." The sound of her voice was small. Everything in the room seemed small.

"Just pack your bags, get out." He reached for her, pulled her to him. "Ana, please."

She stiffened, distracted herself from the feeling that was closing over her. "I want to, but I can't."

She watched him stop what he had started to say, tried to see what he must have been feeling. He let her go, turned his back to her. She tried to focus on the pots in the workroom, how beautiful they were, how different. Some were scorched, still covered in ash. She didn't want to look at him, to see his disgust with her, his hopelessness.

He reached for a vase and inspected it. He had glazed it, robin's egg blue. The rim was fat on one side and thin on the other, tapering down to the bowl. "It's not perfect," he said. "But that's the idea." He held it out to her, an offering.

When she took it, she still couldn't look at him. She wanted to cry, to say the rest of the things still unsaid, that she understood what he meant. She wasn't perfect, and that was all right with him. He was everything to her.

Everything except Emmy. And Frank was in the way. Michael was waiting, hoping she would choose him. If she didn't, he would learn to be alone again. She wondered if he would ever fight for her, if that was what she needed. And it was what she needed, she thought. She didn't know how to fight for herself.

She put the vase down and took his hands, moving them to her face. Without a word, she led him to the bed and made love to him in a slow, bittersweet ritual. It was the only way to tell him the things she could never say. He seemed to understand. He spoke back to her with his body, tenderly, patiently. She watched his face, intent as he kissed her, her feet, her knees, the inside of her legs, and further. His hands found her, centered her, made her head swing side to side, made the little stars behind her eyes burst into color, rocket red, neon yellow, midnight blue. He laid with her, face to face, moving into her, his breath behind her, around her, inside her. He came into her, his head falling back, crying out, a lonely, tortured sound. They slept then, in a warm afternoon, and when she woke, she knew it was too late to stay longer.

When she made herself leave him, she drove slowly toward the city limit, wanting all the while to turn back to him. The feeling left her, quite suddenly, when she saw a white truck a distance behind her. Was it Frank following her? The truck disappeared behind a hill and appeared again, always too far away for her to tell if it was him. It came to her that if she kept on this way, Frank would find out. She was pushing her luck too far. The thought of it made her feel cold and sick. She drove faster, as if her life depended on it, hoping it wasn't him, hoping to have this one last chance. She hardly breathed as she pulled into the driveway at home. There was the tailgate of Frank's truck. It couldn't have been him, after all. She said a prayer of thanks, to whom or what she didn't know–for having evaded discovery, one more time.

At Margaret's place, Ana found Emmy chasing the dogs, pulling their ears and whiskers. And Margaret had helped her make a lumpy basket, decorated with beads and feathers. It was carried home ceremonially, Emmy treating it as a great treasure, and she made sure to put it away in the pillowcase before she would let Ana tuck her in that night.

When Ana climbed into her own bed that night, she again pulled far away from Frank, tucking the quilts tightly around herself, trying to quiet her mind, for sleep. She wished for a storm to distract her, to lull her into sleep. It never rained, but a dry wind picked up, whining, gritty against the windows. It kept her awake long past midnight.

All through March it rained. The Wagon lurched home again and again through the ruts like trenches, through the tire-ripping boulders. Ana resolved to call a meeting-Margaret, Kay and Dean, even Frank, if he would come. They had to do something. She wanted them to work with her, to pitch in their money for repairs, blading, gravel, a culvert for drainage. If they were going to live this way, on this poor excuse for a road, they could at least pay to have it fixed.

The day of the meeting came. Ana met Margaret at Kay's house, Emmy in tow. The VW was dead and buried at the side of the Scudders' driveway. The oil pan had been punctured by a chunk of granite, the suspension system collapsed. Dean was in charge of their only remaining car, the Ranger, and he was in town with it. Frank declined the invitation, heading out to Albuquerque on an errand for his boss. And Henry was in hiding, for once. The Chevy was pulled behind the house, its faded green rump protruding, exposed.

Kay came down the porch stairs, laconic in a green army jacket and blue jeans with holes at the knees. She reeked of marijuana.

"I don't know about you all," she said, throwing a sideways glance at Ana, "but we don't have ten bucks to chip in." She pushed greasy bangs from her forehead and looked at Ana, but her eyes didn't connect. They were vague, indifferent. "Anyway, can't Frank get a backhoe from work?"

"Forget Frank," Margaret said.

Ana ignored her, pleading with Kay. "Don't you want to get your car hauled out, get it fixed? Have a real road?"

"Screw it," Kay said. She pulled a tarnished cigarette case from a pocket and lit a joint. "Maybe I'll get a horse."

Emmy tugged on Ana's skirt, a yellow silk wraparound from Louise. It was too big, pinned in to hold it on, and the pin was coming loose, jabbing her in the side.

"I wanna go home," Emmy whined. She looked like a deranged vagrant, gripping the sock monkey in one hand, and in the other, that filthy pillowcase she wanted to take with her everywhere she went.

"Not yet," Ana said. She was annoyed, frustrated. She thought she saw the yellow-brown of a week-old bruise on Kay's cheek. Dean, at her again.

"Mellow out," Kay said. "Don't sweat the road."

Margaret just snorted, but then started hacking, an aborted, bronchial cough.

"Somebody's got to," Ana said. "Have you driven on it lately? Have you seen the pit at the bottom of the hill?" She didn't say what she wanted to: *Don't you care about anything? Why don't you leave him?* Just as quickly she realized what a hypocrite she was. Frank was no better. She told herself to mind her own business, to stick to the subject of the road. "At least we should put some gravel on it," she said.

Kay held in smoke, then let it out slow. "As soon as we work on it, it'll rain again. Then we'll be back where we started." She started to twist her wedding ring around and around on her finger, as if it was too tight. "What's the point?" she said.

Ana knew it was hopeless. And in a way, she knew Kay was right. But she wasn't giving up. Not yet. "You can't chip in ten bucks?" she added.

"I could," Kay said, "but I'd have to ask Dean for the money. And I'm not going to. But *you* can. *You* ask him."

There were sounds through the trees, a house door slamming, a car door opening. Ana saw Henry's shirt, a bright orange filtered through the trees, shoehorning himself into the Chevy, then plowing out of the driveway. He had to stop to open the gate. It was harder than ever to open it these days, as it was scarred and crumpled at the center, as if someone had rammed it, on purpose.

Margaret looked like she was going to laugh, watching him drag the gate open, steel scraping rock. Then she reached into a pocket, pulled out a twenty, and handed it to Ana.

"Hang onto it in case anybody else around here ever decides to give a shit." She threw a flat-eyed glance at Kay and turned to leave. She walked to the middle of the road and stood, one arm raised, a thick middle finger shot upward, a salute to Henry's retreat. He didn't get out of the car again to shut the gate. He gunned it instead, the Chevy emitting a rude fart of dirty exhaust from the tailpipe.

Ana turned away, almost laughing, then realized that Emmy had vanished. She started to ask Kay if she knew where she went, but Kay wasn't there either. Clearly, the meeting was over. She would give Margaret's money back. Without more, it was of no help at all.

Margaret helped her search for Emmy. She didn't come when they called. They kept calling, searching the road, behind Kay's house, among the trees, and still she didn't come. There was no sign of her until Margaret spotted movement underneath the wooden porch at the front of Kay's house. Emmy was crouched there with Dooby, intent on a stack of twigs she'd gathered and stacked, like firewood.

"What are you doing?" Ana asked, peering through the slats near a broken place where she must have squeezed through.

"I'm making a cookout."

"Why didn't you come when we called?"

"Dooby doesn't want to go."

"I thought *you* wanted to go."

"No, I want to stay here."

Ana resolved to appease her. "We'll have a cookout when we get home."

"Promise?"

"Sure," Ana said.

"Could I light the fire?" Emmy's eyes were wide, excited.

"We'll see," Ana said.

Emmy was acting strange lately, as if she was mad at something, or someone. Ana had no clue what it was about. She seemed to have gotten used to staying at Margaret's. And maybe that's what it was-Margaret. There were all the weird things Emmy had picked up from her. Just the night before, when Ana had come home exhausted from work, Emmy had made an unfamiliar command, the eyes narrowed like Margaret's: "Little Snake wants dinner." Frank had laughed. He'd missed what was behind it, the nickname Margaret must have given her when she got out of line, the demanding ways she'd learned from him.

Ana suspected that Margaret had begun to love Emmy, without even knowing it. She had taught her how to weave baskets, starting with a circle of willow, winding the tender shoots around and around, tucking in feather and bone, beads, ribbons of soft doeskin, until there was a wedding or burden basket. And she was protective. Almost too protective. Emmy complained that she couldn't do anything without her constant and watchful eye. Ana wasn't sure how Emmy felt about Margaret, but at least she wasn't afraid of her any more. Once Emmy told Ana that Margaret was Changing Woman, the one who was there at the biggest flood of the world, the one who rode a sea of water on an abalone shell, to save the world. And when there were no children left at all, Emmy said, she made children from the sun.

12

$\mathscr{A}$na left Emmy with Margaret, again. She found Michael at home, followed him to the workroom.

"I haven't seen you much at the hospital," she said.

"It's been busy," he said. He was forced to meet her eyes, though she could tell he didn't want to. He was trying to sound casual, conversational, but she knew things had changed between them. She heard her own voice-tense, drawn in, the words measured out one by one.

"I love you, Michael."

"We've gone over this," he said. His voice was gentle, but distant, as if he no longer understood her.

She reached for him, as he had for her those few months ago, touching his arms, his fingers. He was forced to meet her eyes, and he shut his own, as if in pain.

"You shouldn't have come," he said.

"I have to see you," she said. "Don't you want to see me?"

He didn't answer for a long time. When he finally did, he opened his eyes to hers again. "I don't think I should keep seeing you, as long as you're with Frank."

"I don't know what's wrong with me," she said. "I don't love him. I love *you*. But I'm afraid."

"You need to leave him," he said again.

She wanted to give him what he was looking for, something that could explain how Frank could have had so much power over her. He wasn't going to listen until she said something that made sense. Something that could change the fact that she'd cheated him. That life itself had cheated him. Her throat felt rough, thick. She drew in as much breath as she could. The words came out labored, as if she was starved for air.

"I'm afraid," she said. "Of what he might do."

"And you think you're safe now?"

"He doesn't know-I don't know-" She searched for a sign that there was anything she could do or say that would make him understand.

He surrendered to her when she pulled him closer, his knees buckling, kissing her softly, then no longer softly. The room changed, there was the bed, she felt the warmth of his throat and wetness, tears, hers, his, she didn't know. He kept drawing her down, he wouldn't be satisfied with her cries until it was agony, and the climbing began again and still she wanted to scream, swelling with the knowledge of what she was gaining, losing, thrusting away from her. It went on and on, as if he could not come, but finally there was the throbbing that ended it, ended as if it had never begun. He was spent afterwards, as was she. They stayed awake, their hands no longer on one another, but empty, listless.

She watched him as he rolled to his side, the way he gazed out the window, away from her. The image of his face, dark against the window glass, seemed old, haggard.

"I can't leave, Michael. I don't know how." She held out her hand, wanting to touch him. If he hated her, she couldn't bear it. She loved him, would not stop loving him.

"I'd help you, if you wanted me to," he said. His head shifted, as if he might turn to her once more.

"Just wait a while," she said. "I'll figure things out."

He shook his head, then stood, pulled on his shirt and jeans. He knew, she could tell-there was nothing to figure out. No plan. Only that she was going to be true to herself, her hopeless, defeated self, the one who never fought for anything. She felt still inside, a cold, thick quiet, like quicksand.

She was late that night, leaving him. At home, she thought, crazily, of telling Frank where she had been. But she couldn't. He would hurt her. Or Michael. Or both of them. Emmy was asleep on the sofa, the quilt tucked around her chin. Ana wanted to wake her, to lift her up, drive away with her, never come back. But instead, she went back to the living room, sat quietly there. Frank sat in his La-Z-Boy, watching television. When he lit a cigar, she had the urge to stand up, grab it, use it to put out his eyes. The urge passed, as it usually did, and in the end, she did nothing.

◊ ◊ ◊

"It's over," she read. "It has to be." Reading the letter from Michael was like sliding a coffin lid over her soul. He didn't call her again, not even once. The truth was, she knew, he couldn't bear to be with her. She didn't blame him for leaving her. She blamed herself, completely. She wasn't a good mother, and she wasn't honest–with herself or anyone else.

She called in to her supervisor, still lying, saying she was sick, that she'd be taking all her leave. But it was only a way to avoid having to run into Michael at work, knowing he didn't want to see her there. She heard nothing from him. She pictured how he must have looked when he wrote the letter, saw his hands, his chapped, strong, tender hands, as he penned it. He wouldn't have thought of all the excuses she'd given him. That she was afraid, weak, incapable of facing up to Frank. He hadn't needed to say more. Just had to say goodbye, to say she had not given enough, tried enough, loved enough. He had probably written the letter at his kitchen table, or the bench where they'd worked together. The words lay cruelly on the thick gray paper.

She imagined him planning it, while chopping wood, wedging clay, giving his anger back to the earth, to hold for him. He would hold the anger in while he was at work. It would still be waiting for him when he got home. The anger would sleep with him at night, wrapping itself around his heart like the parasitic mistletoe on the juniper trees. It would reveal itself in the pots he made–in crude, squat stoneware, heavy with the weight of their emptiness.

She didn't answer the letter. And he didn't wait for her, or fight for her, not any more. In her heart, she knew he had given up, had decided there was no point in arguing, in understanding the things that held her back. When her leave from work ran out, she sent a letter to the hospital, resigning. All Frank knew was the version she told him. She was tired of working. Emmy needed more attention. She didn't think he'd mind since he never wanted her to work anyway, and she was right. He didn't mind. He said they had never needed her income, they would do just fine.

On days she had to go to town, she avoided the hospital, even the street it was on. There was still no word from Michael. There were only the veiled questions posed by her old coworkers when she was unlucky enough to run into them. The lab secretary with the frowsy gray hair cornered her in a drugstore checkout line.

"I asked Michael what happened to you," the woman said. "He just said you quit. He seemed mad. Was something wrong?" Her eyebrows were raised, waiting. She knew. She judged, like everyone else.

"No," Ana lied. "Nothing." Nothing that anyone could help her with, she thought. Only that the place that had opened within her-that small space she'd allowed her spirit to live in-had closed back in, filling in with the thick, ropy flesh of a scar. A cold, sullen mood crouched over her, like an incubus-a sickening, gray spirit. Her mother called often, hinting that she knew how dull and brittle Ana was, how she was wasting away, how she seemed to need something from someone, anyone.

"Just come home," Louise pleaded. "I don't know what's wrong with you", she said, "but I'll help you, whatever it is."

For once, Ana realized, her mother was reaching out, offering help. She wanted to reach back, but the bones in her arms wouldn't move. There was no sinew, no will, to push them up. "I can't," she answered. She was too flawed to receive this kind of love, too much like her father. She didn't deserve it. Besides, she'd never been there for her mother. Even at birth she'd appeared out of the fog of a drug-induced labor, howling, her mother said, like an angry troll. She'd become her father's child. Her mother had been left alone.

Ana held the receiver in both hands, gently. She had never understood her mother before. Now she was beginning to. At the end of that line was a woman like herself, a failed woman, wanting to offer more, to do better.

"Mama," she said, trying to say more, but the words stuck in her throat.

"What is it, Ana? What can I do?"

"I'm okay, Mama. Don't worry."

"I'll pick you up. You and Emmy can stay with me."

"I'm all right here."

"Why won't you let me help you?"

Ana could hear her quiet sobbing. "I'll be okay, really." She thought she heard another sob, then "Call me if you need me."

"I will," Ana replied. She meant what she said, but in truth, she couldn't bring herself to call anyone. She didn't want to talk about anything. She wanted to be alone with the sadness, the heaviness, the feeling that the universe spun indifferently around her. There were no hands to hold her heart to its center, no voice to reach down to open it, to pull her spirit back into being.

In April she found the skis Margaret had given her. They were tied together with a bungee cord, leaning against the wall of Frank's tool room. She remembered the day Margaret had brought them. How wonderful it had been to latch them on, to take her first gliding steps in the snow. Frank had put his foot down, since then. He'd made up a new rule. No skiing, he had said. Too dangerous.

She felt the backs of them, the wax coating scored and pitted from the wear and tear of too many rocks, too little snow. She hoisted them under her arm, carried them out, wedging them into the back of the Wagon. She drove halfway up the road and pulled into the driveway of the Scudder's house. Construction supplies lay scattered around a new room they were building. There were half-empty cement bags, nails, paint buckets. Dean was out there somewhere. Ana could hear him hammering.

Kay answered Ana's knock, holding the door only halfway open. "What's up?" she asked.

Ana hadn't talked to her since the meeting about the road. She felt suddenly self-conscious, uncertain about how the gift would be received. "I just thought..." she paused, wondering how to explain it, then came out with it. "I thought maybe you could make some use of these." She handed her the skis.

Kay's eyes widened. "For...?"

"Not for now," Ana said. "For next winter. When it snows enough to cover the rocks."

"Don't you want them?" Kay asked. She had one hand over her eyes, shielding them from the brilliant glare of the afternoon sun.

"No," Ana said. She turned away before Kay could say more, or argue. It was Margaret who had given her that first taste of freedom, the day she'd brought them over. It was the first time she'd openly stood up to Frank, or at least held her ground. She didn't want to see them again. She didn't let herself cry. She practiced holding it in, holding her breath. It seemed like the only answer, to not care. She felt the rock in her chest, molten, turning. It would cool in time, she thought. She would let go of it, forget it was even there.

13

*I*n spring the weeks turned to a tedious emptiness, a void that made Ana dream of Michael, always waking with a start, as if trying to stop a fall. But she did the best she could to make things seem normal. She bought a cheap pink and white cake for Emmy's fifth birthday and made a ceremony of lighting the candles. She spent days reading to Emmy at the library, carrying picnics to the ridge, taking her to Margaret's where they wove baskets together, wedding baskets, burden baskets, with tin jingles, beads, feathers. Margaret boiled eggs in a pot on her tiny stove and they peeled and ate them, sent Emmy to gather more.

In June, she planted flower seeds: cosmos, flax, aster. She hoped they'd come up in July, thinking how pretty they'd look, blooming in spite of the rocky earth. She filled the watering can in the sink one morning, early, and checked on Emmy before leaving the house. Emmy was in her room, still asleep, but fully dressed. Frank must have forgotten to change her into pajamas. Ana made a mental note to talk to him about it. Children needed to have their routines-unchanged, predictable. She called to her quietly, making sure she wasn't awake, then went outside, carrying the water.

She worked her way across the ridge, dribbling streams in the places she'd planted, trying to remember every one. Halfway through the work, it started raining, and she heard Margaret's dogs, a cacophony of barks and howls. She thought she must have set them off, but then there was distant shouting. The air seemed gray, soft. Then she realized it. There was smoke, unmistakable, somewhere. The road? The house? She faced the house and began to run. She didn't think about the panic that entered her, the water can falling from her hands, the lump at the base of her throat, her heart thudding in time to the pounding of her feet. Wherever the fire was, it could spread. She ran up the steps, slammed the front door open, and raced down the hall. Emmy was not in her room. She shot through the living room, the kitchen, her own bedroom, calling. Emmy was not in the house. Smoke billowed to the sky. No, she said to herself, though no words came out. No, no, no.

She rushed to the flames, eyes wild. "Emmy!" She saw no one, but recognized the place. It was burning. One of the places Emmy went to play. "Emmy!" She tried to keep from dropping to her knees. She whirled to find someone, anyone. Three or four trees were consumed by fire, closer and closer to the house. Then she realized it. A fire truck was making its way up the road toward her, slowly. She stared as it crawled up the road, one boulder at a time, then looked back to the house. Surely, Emmy must be home, after all, sleeping in one of her hiding places. She ran back to the house, through rooms that blurred together as she searched them again-bathrooms, the kitchen, bedrooms. She found a hammer and bashed the doorknob of Frank's tool room off when she couldn't open it, still calling. The room was empty, silent. She gasped for air in short, painful swallows. Her limbs felt heavy, but she forced them to the road again.

Cinders floated above her head. She started screaming, and would have kept on, if not for Margaret, who stepped out from behind her, touching her. Only then was she able to open wild eyes to the miracle at her back. Emmy. The child stood trembling, clinging to Margaret's leg. Her hands clutched the ragged pillowcase, its contents sagging at the bottom, all her secrets. She looked guilty as hell. Ana collapsed into her, clutching, crushing her in her arms.

"Where have you been?" The tears welled up and fell, slipping down her cheeks and nose, running into Emmy's hair.

"With me," Margaret said, and nodded, as if to punctuate it. As if to reassure Ana there had been no reason for her fear.

She couldn't speak, and no one else seemed to want to talk. Not

Emmy, who clung to her like she had as an infant. Not Margaret, whose eyes for once were set wide open, the flames reflected in them like molten lava.

A long stretch of trees was burned, completely, despite the men in their yellow slickers and the tanks of water hosed from the road. The earth was scorched, ruined. When Frank came home to find it, she told him it must have been lightning that started the fire. Emmy stayed strangely quiet when he paced the blackened earth, counting the trees.

Ana stayed inside, waiting. She felt a growing sense of guilt-an uncomfortable feeling that her secrets had led to this place-a place where a mother only thought of herself, of her own wants and needs. She thought of her inattentiveness, and strangely, of the fire in the kiln at Michael's house. It melted all but the common clay. It broke the weakest, changing what was left into glass and stone. *She* was weak. Something must change, or she would be broken.

◊ ◊ ◊

Ana went to Margaret's alone one morning while Emmy was still asleep. Margaret didn't answer the door, so Ana opened it and called to her.

"Come in." Margaret's voice came to her, thin and hollow, down the narrow hallway.

Ana navigated through the cats and into a dark bedroom. She saw it now. The lovely moon-face was still round, but it was yellow, a color like the shadows cast by the dim lamp behind the bed. There was a smell, too, that she noticed for the first time. Something like a hospital smell. Putrid. Deathly. "You're sick," she said.

"So they say." Margaret coughed. She managed a weak smile. Sardonic. Resigned.

"What's wrong?" It was beginning to make sense, the squalor of the place. Margaret *was* too tired, as Emmy had said. Something was terribly wrong. And maybe this was what made her finally give in, confess to Ana what she'd never said before.

"A tumor," she said. "On my kidney."

Ana disguised her shock, making her mouth form a question, buying time. "What do the doctors say?"

"You know how they are," Margaret said. "They say I have choices. I can start giving up body parts and do chemo, or leave it alone."

"What are you going to do?"

Margaret sighed. "Oh, I said they could take it out. They're going to deliver it in a few weeks, like some big, sad baby. I picture it like some evil ghost baby, with some hair and teeth, a piece of gut."

"Margaret–"

"I know. Weird, huh."

"That's not it. I want to help." Ana felt herself on the verge of hysteria, as if she was going to start yelling any minute. Why was Margaret so stubborn? What the hell was wrong with her? Didn't she know she was supposed to let someone know what was going on, that she was supposed to get help? She held the tip of her tongue between her teeth, and waited.

"You could feed the animals." Margaret sounded sad, as if for the first time, she'd thought of something she couldn't handle alone.

"I will," Ana said. "Can I drive you to the hospital, when you go?"

"That would be good." Margaret winced, as if it pained her to accept the help.

"Why didn't you tell me?" Ana made herself sound calm.

"I didn't want to bother you. Anyway, we don't tell each other everything."

Ana felt her face go hot. She knew this, but she felt ashamed, knowing it was her own fault. She'd never taken the time, never slowed down enough to ask, to pay attention. She was going to make up for it now.

"What don't you tell me?"

"Slow down," Margaret said. Not so fast. It'll take time. How much time do you have?"

Ana didn't know what she meant. To Margaret, there was always plenty of time. Ana had never heard her say she was too busy for anything, or that she didn't have time. She thought about it, hard, knowing that there would be a right answer, and a wrong one. If Margaret meant how much time she had today, she had all the time in the world. If she meant some kind of serious time, there was Emmy to think of, her housework, and yes, Frank. There wasn't much time, when she thought about it.

"I'll make time," she said, not knowing what kind of promise it was, or if she could really keep it.

"Good," Margaret said. "You'll need it. I'm going to tell you some things now, so you'll know, in case I die."

"You're not going to die," Ana said.

Margaret ignored this comment, waving her hand as if dismissing Ana's hope, or denial. "I wouldn't have told you before," she said. "But now I have to." The hands worked themselves, but her expression was calm. She closed her eyes.

Ana waited, wanting to ask her what she meant. But she knew Margaret would make everything clear, in her own good time. In fact, Margaret was already talking, more than Ana could ever remember her talking before. If she'd thought she was going to go home any time soon, she now realized it wasn't going to work that way. She settled, uncomfortably, into the lumpy cushion of Margaret's recliner. She folded her hands in her lap, determined not to interrupt.

"Where's Emmy?" Margaret reached over the side of the bed to the brown tabby, who was starting to purr. He jumped on the bed, settled himself against her shoulder.

"With Frank," Ana said. "She's all right."

Margaret sucked in her breath. "She wanted to come over today. We were going to make a wedding basket."

"It's fine," Ana said. "She's fine. Don't worry."

Margaret's brown, slitted eyes rested on her only dimly, but there was something new in them. "I'm going to tell you about Ray. About Ray and the baby," she said.

14

"I was sixteen when I met him," Margaret said. "I walked the roads of the rez day and night, hanging out with friends, staying out all hours at the dances. My grandmother yelled at me, told me no good girl acted like that. Told me next I'd be drinking on the Feast Grounds, if I didn't watch it. But I kept going out, even when Grandmother got a weakness in her side. Only Uncle Wendell fought with me then. But he had his hands full, cutting wood all day. Bringing in deer and turkey, so we'd have something to eat. He finally gave up on me, let me do what I wanted."

Margaret seemed more tired than ever. Ana was beginning to believe she might die, after all. It was unthinkable, but possible. She determined to remember this story, these words. In case she was the only witness.

"Tell me about Ray," she said.

"Ray. Yeah. Ray." Margaret had a faraway look in her eyes. There was just the ghost of a smile on her lips. "Somebody brought him to one of the dances when he was on leave from the Army," she said. "Everybody stared at him. He looked so good in that uniform he was wearing. Sharp. Who knows why he did that-join the Army. Go fight in a jungle when he'd never even seen one! Crazy. But he did look good. I stared at him too, and he saw me. Everybody else was teasing him, calling him 'Mutton,' cause he was Navajo. He didn't care. He just laughed in this nice way, so funny for such a big man. I went off with him later, where my girlfriends couldn't see. They knew the way I looked at him. They tried to tell me what Grandmother would have said. That he wasn't one of us. I went with him anyway.

Grandmother was mad. Then I said I wanted to marry him, and it got worse. It was 'no.' That's all she would say. I was too young. There was no money for a wedding feast. I locked myself in a shed and wouldn't come out. I wouldn't eat or drink. After a while, she and Uncle gave in. They said if I would just come out of that shed, I could do what I wanted.

We had the wedding in the canyon. Uncle found the money for the feast, or somebody pitched in. Anyway, I wore the traditional clothes, and he wore his uniform. We were a pair. I married him all right. He was the most handsome man I had ever seen. We were going to live on a farm his family had. He would stay there with me until they called him back from furlough.

When I left Grandmother and Uncle, I saw the mountains out the back window of Ray's pickup getting smaller and smaller. After a while, down Highway Three, there was a place with cottonwoods and a pond. That was the house we were going to live in. There was a well, a stock tank, a house with four rooms and a porch. There was a chicken coop, a windmill, a barn. Ray picked me up and carried me in the front door. I was happy. I thought I had everything."

Ana got a glass from the kitchen, brought water for Margaret to drink. She sipped it, shifted her body so the bed creaked in protest. "I'll tell you how it was before he had to go away."

"Okay," Ana said. "Tell me all of it. Don't leave anything out." She took the glass back, stuffed a pillow behind Margaret's back.

"He fed the chickens for me," Margaret said. "He'd tell me to stay in bed, to stay warm. He'd be the one to get dressed when it was still freezing outside. He'd put on his boots and go out there. He didn't care if it was snowing or not. He'd come back in and warm his feet in between mine, and I'd smell that corn mash on his hands. He'd talk about how he was going to fix up a little heater for the baby chicks, and I'd laugh at how soft he was. But he really did that once, when it got so cold. When I found out about it, I couldn't believe the barn hadn't burned down. He'd rigged up a kerosene heater with a little tent around it, all the chicks inside. He laughed at me. Said I worried too much. Said I should just think about all the good eggs we were going to have when those little chicks grew up, and said he'd scramble them for me, with bacon and chile. Asked didn't I want to help him pick some prickly pears and make some jelly, so we could have that on some bread. Before long he'd have me laughing and we'd be rolling around like puppies. That's how it was, sweet like that. I thought it would be like that forever, until he started to talk about 'until.' 'Until I have to go away,' he said. 'Until' seemed like 'never' to me, since I had him and didn't know what all that meant. But I learned soon enough."

"He got called up for duty?" Ana asked.

"Duty." Margaret said. "I guess you could put it that way." He got called. They said they were shipping him out, to some place farther away than I'd ever heard of, Vietnam. I couldn't even think of what he would do out there, on the other side of the world. Even when he tried to explain it, that he was a medic, that he helped the men when they got hurt. I asked him why, over and over, like I'd never heard him explain it before. I thought it was crazy, that he should just tell them no. Said his place was to stay home with me and the little chickens whose legs had grown long and whose feathers had turned color. I was proud, even though I'd laughed at him, that he'd saved them through the winter. I thought he *could* tell them no, if he wanted to. No matter how he explained it, I didn't understand. I started crying and begging then, and that was bad. It made him cry, too, when he had to leave."

Margaret's eyelids fell, hiding. There was something too horrible to speak of with eyes wide open. Then she opened them again.

"He left," Ana said. She could tell where this was going. Margaret had been left alone, wounded beyond repair.

"He was killed in nineteen sixty-seven," Margaret said. "They sent me a flag, to remember him by. I ripped it up. I used the pieces as rags to clean the shit on the henhouse floor. Then my stomach started to get big, with a baby I hadn't known I was going to have. I couldn't get down on my knees any more to clean, I got so big. So I burned all those rags in a barrel at the back of the house."

Margaret raised her arms out of the covers and up, toward the low ceiling of the motor home, stretching them out. Then she laid them back down on the bed, palms up, weary. "The air was clear the night I went into labor," she said. "The stars outside my window were so close I wanted to reach out and touch them. I thought if I could touch just one, Ray would show up, to help me."

Ana thought of the hopeless incantations women make when they are in love. She thought of all Frank lacked in the ability to make a woman happy-the tenderness, the ways of men like Ray, like Michael. She studied Margaret's eyes, focused within. "Did you hear from him?" she asked.

"Sometimes," Margaret said. "When the letters got through. But mostly, they didn't. After a while, I had to tell myself he wouldn't get home any time soon, much as I wanted him to. And then I sent word for a midwife, and she came. Juanita-a *partera*, they called her. She came from a village in the canyon, about a mile and a half from the house. She was old, with lines and wrinkles everywhere, all over her hands and face. She had a rosary and she started to pray when she came in, touching the beads and boiling water, cleaning the big enamel pans. She prayed for me to be all right, for my baby to be all right. She prayed to Saint Martin, to no-one I'd ever heard of. She prayed to God, to Maria, to anyone who would listen.

My water broke after she had made everything ready. I started crying and confessed to her-I had no money to pay. She said not to worry, that I didn't have to pay. She helped me, telling me to push, massaging me with olive oil. When the baby's head started to show, she took a clean white rag and used it to hold her, to keep her from coming out too fast. And then she came out, and Juanita got to hold her, cleaning her face, helping her breathe. She tied the cord with one string, and then another, farther out, then cut in the middle. And then she wrapped her in a blanket-my baby, Christine. I named her for Grandmother."

She took a deep breath and raised a hand to her heart, pressed her lips together.

"Are you all right?" Ana asked. She reached to her, to hold her hand.

"Let me finish," Margaret said. She squeezed Ana's fingers, held on to her.

Ana didn't feel ready to hear the rest of it. There was nothing good at the end of this story, she knew. But she gave in, nodded. "Tell me."

"I talked to her from the start," Margaret said. "Told her how straight her back was, how black her hair. I fell in love, right then. I let her nurse. Juanita put a binder on me, a long straight piece of cloth, to help with the cramping. After a while, she said she was going to go. I was so grateful to her for helping me. I told her to take one of the hens for her pay. She said she would, but I know she didn't. They were all still there when I went to feed them.

The baby grew. I couldn't believe we'd survived, that we hadn't died. I thought we would, because we were alone. I ended up trading eggs for seeds-sugar corn, beans, pumpkins. I planted and watered and they grew, and we had food in the garden. Christine learned to climb the kitchen stairs, the bed where I had slept with Ray. I helped her learn to walk, pulling her up so she could stand, holding her hand, letting her legs get steady. I took her along when I got kindling for the woodstove, or when I went to get the sumac for my baskets. When all her teeth came in, she learned to roll a piñon nut inside her mouth, to crack the shell. I made her a corn silk doll out of a green husk, using the silk for the hair.

I started to make baskets again, like Grandmother taught me. I made burden baskets, with black from devil's claw, on white cottonwood. I made my own designs, and some I remembered-people, dogs, butterflies. I cut the jingles myself, out of Clabber Girl baking powder tins. I started to sell the baskets at the rodeos, and things got better."

Ana was afraid to say much. She wondered what had happened to the baby, wondered that a woman could have so much, be robbed of so much.

"You were brave," she said, "to do it all alone."

"I told myself everything was good. I didn't have to be lonely, as long as I had Christine. I started believing again, like I had when Ray and I were first married, that I had everything I would ever need."

Margaret had barely come up for air. Ana felt she, too, was out of breath, that she was going to drown if there was no relief, no happy ending.

"It rained the morning it happened," Margaret started.

She leaned over to pull out a picture in a small wooden frame, from a bag at the side of the bed. It was a faded photograph, of a girl not more than three or four-in a white dress-standing at the side of a plain dirt road. Margaret went on, and it seemed she was talking more to the photograph than to Ana.

"I was at the barn, milking the cow. I thought Christine was asleep.

But I could see the house from where I was–I thought I was keeping an eye on everything. We had those old cottonwoods. There'd been a thunderstorm, and their trunks were wet, black from the rain."

She paused, shutting her eyes. "I was almost finished when I walked by the pond. She was floating there, face down, her little gown..." She stopped, let her head rest in her hands, the tips of her fingers pressed into the bone above her eyes. "She was only four years old." She let go of Ana's hand, finished the story. I had to pull her in with a long tree branch. She was still soft. But cold."

If ever Ana was to see Margaret cry, she thought, it would be now. Everything about her seemed ready for it–the eyes, wet and shiny, the hands tense, gripping the blankets. But she didn't. She just took in the small amount of air her lungs allowed her to swallow, and went on.

"She never woke up."

Ana reached for her again, held on to her hands.

"I cried–Aye-yaaa," Margaret said. "I wept and wailed. I cut off all my hair, and tied the ends in a rag, hanging them in a tree in the forest, where no one would find them. Everything that belonged to her, I burned. The officials made me bury her in the cemetery, but still, I wrapped her body in doeskin, and I found a big white stone from a cliff nearby, to mark that grave. I sang a special song for her, to appease her ghost. I wandered off, after they put her in the ground. I said to myself I would never let that happen again, to put someone I loved in that cold, hard ground.

I tried to dry my tears. I made myself go on. I saved all my money, and with that, I bought the motor home, the first place that ever really belonged to me. I traded a rodeo rider all the chickens for his promise to hitch the motor home to his truck and pull it to La Cueva. I put a down payment on the lot and set up shop for my baskets. I built a new chicken coop and settled in. I buried my memories of Ray, of my baby. I thought, somehow, I could kill the pain by not thinking of them, ever again."

Ana searched Margaret's face for tears, and finding none, bowed her head, and wept. If Margaret couldn't cry, she would do it for her, for both of them.

15

t the back of the house in a clear space between the trees, Ana showed Emmy how to cut the eyes out of old, wrinkled potatoes and how to push the pieces wet side down into the spongy earth. They watered them every day with Ana's water pail and Emmy's yellow beach bucket. By July the potatoes were growing. New potatoes, little ones, their soft, fat leaves weaving from the mossy lumps of ground.

"Momma, come see!" Emmy ran inside, panting, spattering dirt on the kitchen floor.

"What?" Ana asked. She was busy folding clothes, hanging Frank's shirts on the back of the door. Emmy pulled her by the wrist out the back door and down the steps. She ran ahead to the trees where they'd planted the small garden and came back out holding handfuls of baby potatoes, the spindly roots threaded between her fingers like matted hair. Ana followed and knelt with her there, digging tunnels in the dirt with her bare hands. The crop had grown wild. They dug the potatoes up and ate them for days, steamed, drenched in butter, sprinkled with salt and pepper.

"Are there any left?" Ana asked as they headed, once again, for Emmy's swing.

"Ssshh! You'll scare them," Emmy whispered. She tiptoed, piñon cones crunching beneath her sneakers.

"What? The potatoes?"

"No, silly! The fairies!"

Ana laughed softly. "What fairies?"

Emmy's eyes flickered. "I saw them, but you can't," she said. She didn't seem to like it that Ana had laughed. She knelt, parting the branches of a cedar, showing Ana another clearing inside a grove. Then she climbed in and sat on well-packed earth, peering out at Ana from the green-armed trees as if she was a fairy herself.

She must have come here many times, Ana thought, following, crouching to join her. A secret place. In Emmy's hair there was a silver-gray twig snagged in the tangles. Her face seemed narrower to Ana. Older. She wondered where Emmy had gotten the clothes she was wearing. She didn't remember the too-big paisley shirt, the faded blue pants, the red plaid patch at the knee. The clothes must have come with the last sack of hand-me-downs sent from Louise. And Emmy must have chosen these herself in the morning when she got dressed. No ruffles and smocking for this girl, Ana thought. But it was all right. She was who she was.

"You like it here, Momma?"

"It's nice." Ana breathed in the warm cedar air.

Emmy pulled Ana's hand to a cool, flat rock and pressed it there. "This is where they dance," she said. "You could hear them sing. Listen."

Ana sat all the way down. "What are they singing?"

Emmy didn't hesitate. "*Summertime.*"

"Hmm." Ana stilled the impulse to smile. "I wonder where they learned that?"

"From you. When you used to sing."

It was so good, Ana thought, to pay attention to Emmy. To singing, living.

"They want to be alone now," Emmy croaked.

"Okay," Ana whispered, and followed her.

Emmy stopped by the swing. It hadn't been used for months. "Will you swing me?"

Ana remembered the laundry waiting to be finished. She usually tried to do it all before Frank got home. She let the thought slip away.

"Sure, hop up." She stayed for a long time, pushing her in the swing. She sang the old songs from her father's records and some songs he never had. When she couldn't remember the words, she just hummed. All the while, Emmy rode the swing like a chariot, singing with her, laughing in tight, loopy squeals that echoed through the trees.

◊ ◊ ◊

They settled in to drive the road again, Emmy buckled down in the back seat, Margaret next to Ana with a blanket and a pillow. They were headed for Ruidoso, for the Changing Woman ceremony.

"Are you sure you're strong enough for this?" Ana asked.

"I'm sure," Margaret said.

They were going to find some miracle for Margaret, something to heal her. Margaret said she didn't care, that she had made her peace with dying. But Ana hadn't.

It was quiet for a while, with only the sound of the Wagon's tires on asphalt. They'd spent themselves on talk of Frank and how he'd discouraged them from going, how Ana had pulled out of the driveway in spite of him. They'd talked of Margaret's tests in the hospital, of what procedures would be done when they got back. Now they settled in, watching the scenery, south to Duran, through flat lands. Clouds reached through the air like fingers of angel hair, then gathered together like silver-white sponges in a sea of blue. Duran flashed past like the pop of an old-style camera bulb and was gone. There was only an abandoned stone grocery, a collapsed building of rotted wood and corrugated metal. Then there was nothing but land again. Emmy broke the silence for a while, counting the cars that passed. Fords, Hondas, an old Econoline. By the time they got to Lincoln County Line, she was asleep.

They passed Corona with its peeling billboards, a bar, a rusted out Mobil station. The land turned from flat brown to rolling green. The bright lines of the two-lane highway matched the yellow-petaled black-eyed susans lining wire fences. There was sharp-bladed yucca, new pods shining in peridot-green. A steel windmill mounted on a weathered wooden frame moved the air with rusted blades, and long-stemmed grass bent in a soft wind. In the distance, a slash of lightening split the sky. Sharp raindrops spattered against the windshield, and Ana drove on, still wordless. A lone Cadillac sailed by, long, white, out of place. Telephone poles topped with blue-glass insulators ran for miles, like rain-soaked crucifixes. There was the predictable lone shoe, abandoned at the side of the road.

"Why is there always just one shoe?" Ana asked.

Margaret just shrugged. "One-legged cowboys."

More yuccas grew on the next stretch, tall-standing, with twin and triple clumps of long, thin leaves, like shocks of green hair. One stood taller than all the rest in thick, white-velvet bloom. A train seemed to come from nowhere and ran beside them. Union Pacific and Santa Fe. Not much of a train. Miles of flatbed trailers with no box cars. Gourd plants turned their sharp leaves upward, drinking in a rain that had turned soft, serious. The land humped into flat-topped hills, long streaks of sandstone, layered, brown sand, red earth.

Hours later signs of civilization finally began to reappear. Mailboxes cropped out every few miles in aluminum-foil silver, enamel black. Carrizozo came into view with its mission style buildings, the arching stone facades leaning out over the narrow roadway.

Ana checked the map, but Margaret stopped her. "I know the way," she said.

They passed the intersection of highways 380 and 54. An abandoned restaurant at Carrizozo boasted "Packaged Liquor – Drive-Through or Lounge Service." They were closer. The mountains came into view, like sleeping dinosaurs. The Guadalupe, Oscura, Three Sisters, the Sierra Blanca that towered over all of them. Ana saw that Margaret was asleep now too, her face pale and damp against a pillow wedged between the seat and the window. They passed a plywood likeness of Smokey Bear, shirtless, with Ranger's hat, blue jeans, his trusty shovel. "Only you can prevent forest fires," the sign said. On the last stretch into Ruidoso the highway was lined with cedar-shingled A-Frames, storefronts selling pottery, leather goods, the TeePee Café, the Roy-El Saloon. And just as quickly as it had appeared, the town faded away. After one last turn, a forest of ponderosa pines rose above them, ancient, towering. A world of trees.

Wickiups dotted the campground, the pine and oak-framed shelters newly constructed, woven with oak leaves for shading. Some had blue tarps on top to keep out the rain. Ana picked an area reserved for tourists, shady and cool. There was the smell of wood smoke and the damp air wrapped them like a soft, warm sheet. Ana pitched the tent with Emmy's help, driving in stakes, putting in poles, piling in the sleeping bags and blankets. And then there were the last few coughs and sneezes of a community gathered to rest before a celebration. Emmy and Margaret were the first to curl down in the musty flannel of the sleeping bags, and they fell asleep while Ana fussed over them, trying to keep them warm.

Later, in the darkness, Margaret whispered. "Are you still awake?"

"Uh huh," Ana said.

"Will you make me a promise?"

"What?"

"When I die, don't let them put me in the ground."

"You're not going to die," Ana said.

"I mean it," Margaret said. "The thought of Christine in the ground. So lonely. Throw my ashes to the east, near that big ponderosa."

"All right. If that time comes, I promise," Ana said, and then she let herself cry silently until she fell into sleep.

At six in the morning Emmy solemnly shook them awake. She held a flashlight, trained on their eyes.

"Wake up," Emmy said.

"Coffee," Ana grumbled, rolling to the side.

Margaret pulled herself up, shivered, gathered a blanket around her shoulders.

"Can I make the fire?" Emmy asked.

"No," Margaret said, casting one of her sharp, slit-eyed glances at Emmy. She grabbed the matches, handed them to Ana.

Emmy hopped on one foot and then the other, shivering. "Can I have hot chocolate?" she asked.

"Sure," Ana said. She lit a match, set it into the kindling. Then she got a metal pan, for water.

Margaret sloughed off the sleeping bag and Ana helped her to a folding chair next to the fire. The campground was still dark, but there were snatches of singing, softly beating drums. There was the high pitch of a lead singer, answered by distant voices. Swallows were just starting to dart in and out of the elms, and the air was wet after a morning rain.

She set the water to boil, then helped Margaret dress. The coffee was poured into insulated orange cups. The smell of sizzling meat was already in the air, with roasting corn and fry bread, coffee, piñon smoke. Children started out from tents and wickiups. Brown girls in pink dresses, sleek-haired boys in long shirts and baseball caps. It was just as Margaret explained it to Emmy, and she told her what to do. "Don't jump around when you're watching," she said. "You have to be still."

"Why?" Emmy asked.

"Because it's serious. Everyone has to be quiet."

Emmy nodded, somber, watching the men gather in the clearing to hoist the teepee. They stretched it tight over the tall pine poles. The canvas was painted with a sun, moon, stars, and a rainbow. All the while Margaret was explaining everything. She'd already answered a hundred questions, but she didn't seem tired.

Families gathered at the grounds, some remembering Margaret, stopping to talk, to ask her where she'd been all this time. She shrugged, lied, told them she hadn't been far. They left her alone then, settling themselves on bleachers and around the center of a packed earth circle. Ana and Emmy followed Margaret, walking slowly up a narrow trail.

They watched as the first young maiden stepped to the center of the ceremonial grounds, head down, hands held together near her waist, humbly. She wore a buckskin robe, with long fringe and tin bells. A cattail drinking tube hung from around her neck.

"Her lips can't touch water," Margaret whispered. "If they do, it could rain."

The abalone shell was placed against the girl's forehead, and she made four runs around the sacred basket that held the powers for her well-being: pollen, ocher, a deer-hoof rattle, a bundle of grama grass.

More women appeared, wearing gathered skirts and long-sleeved tops in a rainbow of vibrant blues, yellows, purples. "That one next to her is the helper," Margaret said. "She'll guide her through the ceremony." Men in the background chanted and drummed. The girl began to move her feet in a deliberate, quick-stepping motion. With every beat, she pounded a long, ochre cane on the ground. The fringe on her dress moved with her, and the bells jingled.

"Every step is a prayer," Margaret said. "For strength, long life, happiness." She herself seemed to be in prayer, her eyes lowered, one hand folded over the other.

The sun crept up into dawn. A blaze of glassy pink clouds swirled across the sky. The girl danced into daylight. And when that was done, she kneeled to reenact the story of the first Changing Woman. She faced the full sun and let it flow into her, taking it in as if she was beginning the world anew.

They moved closer to the circle, watching. The girl stretched out full length, lying still like a lump of clay to be shaped and molded. The woman massaged her as she would a baby, touching her eyes, to make them open, and her mouth. She was shaping her into the woman she was to become. Emmy stood still, holding Ana's hand.

All day long, the drums beat, strong and rhythmic. Ana shut her eyes and felt something rise up in her with each long breath that filled her lungs. There was the old familiar feeling at first, the twisted place at the center of her chest. But there was a new one, too. Circles of fire in her belly, rising, ebbing, turning to a great salt ocean. She felt the shape of Emmy's hand. It grounded her like deep roots in rocky earth. She heard the singer's prayers for plants, for rain, for mountains. Strangely, slowly, she felt the shape of her own soul pulling up from the center. She felt the curve of it, the opening space of it. It came wide open like the mouth of one of Michael's vases, broad and smooth, firm, strong. Inside it was the place where she'd rocked on the water in a canoe with her father, where she'd cradled Emmy in the bend of her arms, in the bed where she'd lain with Michael. She kept still, her eyes closed and her mind quiet. She kept still until the drums faded away, until the singers were silent, until she felt Emmy's small hand again, squeezing her fingers.

The drums beat on into night. The men gathered again, building a fire. They lit pine kindling and it burst into hot orange flame. They added more wood, then larger and larger slabs, then quartered logs the size of beams, straining with the weight. Ana studied Margaret's face. It was the same moon-shape, though thinner. And there was pain in it, of a physical kind. But there was also a look of peace. Ana had never seen that before. Margaret's eyes were shining, like the fire.

In the distance children called to each other. Wood smoke rose to the darkening blue. The Mountain Gods, the *Gah'e*, began to dance, their belts jingling. The tall headdresses rose and fell around the fire, around the clowns that danced wildly behind them. They approached the fire and retreated, and more came, circling in. The bells rang louder and louder, like hard raindrops on a tin roof. They came like the wind, like a rainstorm, making a sound like thunder. The fire sent whirlwinds of bright sparks into a dark sky. The Mountain Gods danced and danced long into the night, thrusting their swords toward the firelight, making things right with the world.

16

*I*n August Frank began to work on the house again, finishing walls, cutting tile, installing glass where windows had been left boarded over. He took out loans, laid tile and thick cream-colored carpet, installed shelves and cabinets. He insisted Ana buy new things-brocade curtains, brass table lamps, and a blue oriental rug. Ana wished it would make her happy, the newness and luxury of it. But she knew that unlike her mother, it was not money or things that gave her satisfaction. Still, she felt she could not complain; even Frank's demeanor had changed. He seemed to draw pride from the work on the house, and behaved differently toward her at times, more solicitous, indulging.

At night, when he reached for her, she thought "not now, not ever." But there was something curiously vulnerable about his pale, naked body. She tried at least to pity him. But she felt ill afterwards, and she turned away as soon as possible, waiting for the aversion to pass. She stayed in bed late in the mornings. In bed she could think, could have time alone, in peace.

The house, she thought, had never become a home. It was a castle surrounded by the moat of the road, and it became clear to her that she had made herself a willing prisoner. One morning as she listened to Frank in the kitchen, the clink of his spoon in his coffee, a sad smile passed across her face. She said aloud, though in a whisper, "I'm through with this."

She wanted to leave immediately. How good, she thought, it would be to pack her things, to go now, this morning! And then she thought how impossible it would be. She would have to confront him, somehow explain, then get Emmy, borrow money from her mother, get a job in town. It occurred to her that there was something else, something within herself that had kept her back, kept her from seeking the kind of life she wanted. Still wanted. A life with Michael.

She got up, still in the slip she had worn to bed, and went to the kitchen. Frank looked relaxed as he had been for the past few weeks, and it gave her courage. She stood behind him, pressing her fingers into the table, as if trying to pull strength from it, from the dark, glossy streaks that ran like a woman's hair through the heavy, oak surface.

"I'll be home at six," he said.

"It doesn't matter," she answered. She said it knowing the meaning that it had for him, for her. But she let go of the fear she had held for so long.

"What do you mean?" He hadn't caught on.

She still had a moment or two to change her mind, to save herself. She didn't. She looked at him straight on, and the words came spilling out.

"It doesn't matter, because I won't be here." It was time to leave him. She hadn't planned out the details, what she would say, how to explain. She had stayed so long, too long. He would never make her happy, and she no longer cared to please him. She stood, still pushing her fingers hard against the table. It was cool to the touch, but unyielding. It seemed to push back toward her, holding her up. She left the table and walked to the piano, ran her fingers tenderly across its red-brown wood. There was music here, music she couldn't bring herself to play, to sing, when Frank was in the room, because he stifled her so.

"What does that mean?"

"It means I'm leaving."

"What?"

She could see she had caught him off guard in the way his head swung back, as if she'd landed a sucker punch.

"I'm leaving you, Frank. Moving out."

Her fingers trailed to the keyboard and she ran them calmly, silently, across the ivory keys.

He shook his head, stunned. "No you're not-"

Ana watched the familiar flush of rage begin, but she went on. "It just doesn't work, Frank. We don't work."

He moved toward her, and she thought he would strike her. Instead, his fists came down on the piano, fast and hard, on the lowest keys, a crashing like rocks breaking, like the ones under the house, the ones buried deep in the mud of the road. It was going to be hard, this leaving, just as she'd always thought. But she wouldn't stop now. She stared at him. His face twisted. He looked like an angry god.

"What the hell does *that* mean?" He leaned in on her again, the eyes bulging, the fists shaking themselves out, then grabbing her arms, squeezing so tight she could feel the bruises forming.

Still, she felt herself rising up, her eyes sliding down on him. She jerked away from him. "Let go of me."

His eyes held some kind of unfocused rage. He didn't let go. "And Emmy? What about her?"

"She's coming with me," Ana said. She returned the glare, willing herself not to tremble, not to weaken.

He became, again, the angry man she had known for so long. His eyes bore down on her, and he was shaking, loose-limbed, as if something in him was about to break.

"You think you're going to find somebody better?" he asked.

Her face flushed, but she held herself steady. "I'm leaving, Frank. It doesn't matter what you say." This time, it was she who was controlled, she who said how things would be.

"Or maybe you already have." He shook her, again and again, until she felt her teeth would break against each other, and still she kept her eyes on his. She felt the crush of his hands as he gripped her arms. She didn't care what he did. He could kill her now if that's what he intended to do. She was ready. It was time to fly.

"There could have been," she said. "But it didn't work out."

His hands fell from her arms, and he turned from her. She backed away from him, waiting, watching him. He seemed to her–suddenly smaller. A wiry, tired-looking man. A stranger in steel-toed boots.

"Get out." He was almost whispering now. Warning her. "When I come back, you'd better be out of here." He slammed outside, wheeled the pickup out of the driveway, and tore down the road, everything clanging, crashing, as if he himself was the force that could heave the earth inside out and crush the rock that held it together.

She packed. Quickly, silently. She threw clothes into boxes and stuffed an old suitcase borrowed from her mother. It was a tan leather case, the frame poking through the worn hide, water-stained. She went to Emmy, lifting her sleep-heavy body. She propped the door open and carried her down the steps and into the Wagon.

The road was dry that night. She drove as if she didn't know where it would take her, as if she didn't care. She pushed the Wagon hard and fast, steering around the ruts and boulders. She thought if she didn't slash a tire on the next rock, she would never have to stop, would drive straight ahead, into the miles of sky, trees, mountains. She left Frank behind, him and the house he'd built. She would be back for Margaret, soon. But for now, she only looked ahead, to the road where it ended–to the post where the gate was propped open, and beyond.

*I*n Margaret's hospital room the clock on the wall was round, like a school clock, with big black numbers. It ticked, loud and slow, and Ana watched the long hand click forward as she pushed the door open to walk in, carrying a bunch of yellow daisies in one hand and a clear vase of water in the other.

Margaret was just coming out of the bathroom, the toilet flushing, all her heft of bones and joints hobbling toward the bed. She leaned into it, wrapped herself into the sheets. "Hey," she said.

"Hey." Ana put the flowers in the vase and set it on the bed tray. She used a napkin to soak up a puddle of water that had spilled, then sat in the vinyl chair beside the bed. "How did the surgery go?"

"Like I expected," Margaret said. "They took out the tumor. Bought me some time."

"Did they get all of it?" Ana knew better. But she couldn't help asking. She was hoping for a miracle.

"No. But there's nothing more they can do. At least they said I could go home."

Ana thought of Margaret alone. She didn't know how she was going to help her, but she had made a decision. She would be there for her, whatever it took. Miraculously, she had landed a full-time job as a social worker for the state since moving out, had found an apartment in town. Taking care of

Margaret would mean continuing to deal with the road, for a while at least, and possibly seeing Frank. But he had agreed, in a series of conversations mediated by one of her friends at work, that he wouldn't bother her except to have her drop Emmy with him on the weekends, and both of them had stuck to the agreement.

She looked around the room at the flesh-colored walls. There was the familiar smell of iodine, floor soap. It was dismal here, as she remembered it. A green curtain hung on rings, separating Margaret from the empty bed on the other side. The tumor must have been vascular, as they'd suspected. Malignant. It made her sick to think about it. She had been heartless over these last months, thinking only of her own disappointments, her own life dramas, her dreams.

"When can you go home?" she asked.

"Tomorrow. Will you check on the animals today?"

"You know I will. And I'll take you home tomorrow."

"Good, then. I have something else to talk to you about."

"What?" Ana asked. "Tell me now."

"No. Best wait till then."

Ana didn't argue. Later, they would talk about these things. "Arrangements," people called them. The things you do when someone is going to die. About what to do with the dogs, the cats, the parakeet, the chickens. She couldn't bear the thought of it.

At Margaret's place the motor home seemed to have rusted more, sunk even more deeply into the earth. The dogs ran along the length of a chain-link fence, bounding, racing. They barked when she stood behind the gate, filling their buckets with water from a hose. They stopped and sniffed, splaying their paws against the mesh of their pens, snuffling, greeting her. By the time she left them to feed the cats, they were competing for her attention, licking her hands, tails swinging.

Inside, the kitchenette was cluttered with soft leather rags, coils of sumac and willow. A wooden shelf held the most precious baskets, beaded and feathered, like tiny birds' nests. There was a familiar smell of coffee and bacon and used cat litter. The cats approached her cautiously, the white one yielding to the fat brown tabby in a silent battle over the kibbles. Ana waited on them, filling their feeders and water buckets to the brim. She wondered which one had broken into the bread bag on the table. There were claw holes in the plastic, a telltale trail of crumbs across the floor.

She was glad to see the parakeet still surviving. The bird chirped and ruffled while she put dishes in the sink to soak. Outside, she scattered cracked corn for the chickens and gathered eggs. She would bring the eggs in, boil them, have them ready for Margaret when she came home. They would peel and eat them together, plain with a little salt, and Margaret would say whatever it was she had left to say.

The next day Ana headed for the hospital again, this time with Emmy. She got Margaret out, rolling her in a wheel chair through the sliding glass exit doors, helping her into the Wagon and buckling Emmy in the back seat. They got through the traffic lights of Santa Fe and on to the highway, then finally to the Laundromat, the junk car lot, the cemetery, the adobe church at Cañoncito, the "It'll Do Motel." She only had to slow down once, for Bernardo's septic tank service truck. Margaret read the bumper sticker out loud: *Your shit is my bread and butter.* It made them laugh.

"Sick," Ana said.

"It's the truth," Margaret said, still laughing.

Ana turned into the road, and Margaret pointed to the gate post. "What's that?"

Ana saw it now-the gate had been ripped off entirely. What was left of it, its smashed steel carcass, was lying in the mud of the ditch. The chain had been cut clear through, the padlock open, hanging on what was left of it.

"Dean must have done it," Margaret said. "The bastard is good for something after all."

"How do you know?" Ana asked.

"I know everything," Margaret said.

"I don't doubt it. Speaking of that, what was it you were going to tell me?"

"Oh that." Margaret looked out the window, away from Ana. "Well, I don't know if you want to hear it."

"Try me," Ana said.

"This nurse I met at the hospital..." Margaret started, and then she trained her slit-eyed glance on Ana's face.

Ana felt her body soften. Had Michael asked about her? Was he thinking of her? She didn't want to talk about it with her. Not now. Not with Emmy here. And Emmy was listening. She could tell from the dead quiet coming from the back seat.

"You know," Margaret said. "That guy nurse." She still stared at Ana, not letting up.

"What about him?" Ana wondered how Margaret could have known about him. He worked on the psych ward–was never on the floor she'd been on.

"I looked him up," Margaret said. "You mentioned him once. Said he was a potter. I was curious."

"Oh," Ana said, nervous, waiting for Emmy's reaction.

"He said you're a fool," Margaret said. "And I agreed."

"Who?" Emmy said.

"No one," Ana said. "Margaret's just kidding."

"Why?" Emmy asked, wriggling forward, grabbing the back of the front seat as if she would catapult herself forward, take over the wheel if she didn't get an answer.

"Because your mom is so silly," Margaret said, reaching back to tickle her, making her laugh until she couldn't breathe.

In La Cueva, after Margaret was settled in, Emmy had exhausted all her energy, had collapsed into a sleepy lump. Ana carried her back to the Wagon, drove back to the apartment, and got her into bed. She couldn't help thinking, once again, of Michael-of what Margaret had said. The phone was at the bedside, and she thought of all the months she had left him alone, as she supposed he wanted. She picked up the receiver and dialed.

"Michael?"

"Ana," he said. His voice was flat, uninterested.

It was hopeless. He hated her. "I thought you might help me, with a friend," she said.

"I have to go-"

"You have to talk to me some time." She was pleading, now. How cold he was, how stubborn.

"I can't, Ana. I won't." He hung up on her.

She dropped the receiver into the cradle. It didn't connect, but she couldn't bear to touch it again. She lay down on the floor. She could hear the tinny recording come on the line. *If you'd like to make a call, please hang up and try again.* She imagined herself vivisected, laid out on a stainless steel table, Frank above her, wielding a scalpel. She'd like to make a call, all right. To Frank, to tell him he had ruined her life. To God, to curse him for what he was doing to her, to Margaret.

◊ ◊ ◊

Ana kept Margaret going. All through September she took her to the hospital, to the drug store, to get groceries. Sometimes Kay helped with the animals, and Ana was grateful. She hated having to drive to La Cueva, having to deal with the road or having to see Frank or Henry, even from a distance. But she kept on, driving the road fast, keeping her eyes trained on Margaret's place. She fed the dogs and cats by the light of kerosene lamps, broke the ice in the water buckets, filled the tubs to the brim so they could make it on their own, if they had to. She cleaned the straw in the coop, gathered eggs, scattered feed, throwing it far so the chickens wouldn't peck at her. Back at home, she kept watch for the time that Margaret could no longer care for herself. Around the edges she dealt with her own life, Emmy, and work.

She fixed her apartment up, decorating it with Margaret's baskets of willow and sumac, dandelion root, elder bark. They lifted her spirits, as things the wind could move, that a woman could use to make something of nothing. Margaret always started her baskets from the emptiness in the center and built in a circle, twining and pressing and winding. She used everything-teeth, hands, fingernails-until a thing of beauty was born, a foundation coiled around a center core, wound with long, smooth splints of the most tender shoots. She remembered how Margaret had laughed when Emmy asked if her Daddy could make a basket like that. "No," she'd answered. "It's much too hard for a man."

Most of the baskets were in the kitchen, with some in the dining nook. There were flat, round wedding baskets, deep burden baskets with tin jingles, curved water bottles, open bowls. The rest of the apartment was filled with odd pieces of secondhand furniture stuffed into rooms with narrow doorways.

There was no room for the piano; Frank had agreed to keep it, until she could find a bigger place. Instead, there was a cheap sofa bought from a second-hand store, a pine dining table with a wobbly leg and mismatched chairs. And in the corner by the sofa hung a bird cage, Margaret's parakeet, the round white head folded under a sky-blue wing, asleep.

One morning, Ana grew tired of lying in bed, sleepless, fretting about the work she had to do the following day. She got up and stumbled, bleary-eyed, to a storage closet. She dug out a rickety card table and a bag of damp clay she'd saved from her days with Michael. The rest of the morning was spent working the clay, punching and pulling until she wore herself out.

The bowl she tried to make was lumpy and crude, no matter how hard she tried to smooth and finish it. She pounded it out, stuffed the clay back into the bag, and went to work the next day, but the thought of it pulled at her, so she returned to it again that night, and again the next day. She found time for it on weekends when Emmy was with Frank, and early mornings on weekdays she folded the clay in on itself, turning it, kneading it like bread dough. A stubborn pride grew in her. It kept her working, making pots by hand at first—rolling long, fat coils and spiraling them in on themselves, walking around them, pinching, pushing, scraping.

After a few weeks, she scrounged a used potter's wheel and started turning them. She had decided; whatever else she was going to do with her life, this would be a part of it. When she saw Margaret, she complained that she didn't know why she dealt with the frustration of it—there was never anything beautiful, as there had been at Michael's.

"Clay is stubborn," Margaret said.

"Like you," Ana laughed.

"Like *you*," Margaret said. "Anyway, it isn't like baskets," she added. "With clay, you have to let it be what it wants to be. It can't be forced."

It was true, and Ana didn't argue. Michael had said that once, too. There was always some tension, a resistance she knew she needed to overcome. She found it hard to let go, to give up the image she had of the pot before she started work on it. And that seemed to make things worse. The walls of her vases turned out too thick or too thin, the handles on cups too fragile. But she never gave up trying. Her hands began to learn to listen to the clay, to hear the right way to squeeze and pinch it into a strong base, into tall slim walls that didn't collapse on themselves. She played with the forms, making bottles, vases, cups, full-bodied bowls with sensual curves. They were simple but sturdy things. She fired them at a ceramics shop downtown, the early pots going in vulnerable, coming out chalky, buckled and cracked. But she learned from her mistakes, the art of controlling the oxygen, the temperature, of waiting for the right time to open the door. Slowly, she began to save more pots than she destroyed.

18

$\mathscr{I}$n October Ana woke early to find Emmy slumbering in her bedroom, looking deceptively angelic. Bills were strewn on the dining room table, a dismembered vacuum cleaner cluttered the living room floor. In the kitchen, the dishes were washed, stacked neatly in their strainer. And in one corner of the dining nook, Margaret, who had finally surrendered to Ana's full-time care, slept on a daybed. Rain had pelted the house the night before–hard enough to force a leak through the ceiling, and it was dripping into a good-sized puddle in the middle of the dining table. It had created a long, cloud-like stain, penetrated so deeply in the pine boards that Ana could not get it out. After ten minutes of futile polishing, she went on to other chores. She swept the dust that had gathered on the floors, folded a pile of clothes, plumped the pillows on the sofa. Then she took on the kitchen, tossing out used paper plates and washing the counters. She smiled to see Dooby, the old sock monkey, staring back at her from a corner shelf with his black-button eyes. Emmy neglected him more and more these days. But just yesterday she'd played with him as in the old days, stuffing his red yarn mouth with chocolate icing from a cake they'd bought for Margaret's birthday. Ana had put him in the wash, watched his helpless body yanked about in the foamy water until he was clean. She had squeezed the water out and put him on the windowsill to dry.

Margaret woke up in a talkative mood, wanting Ana to sit next to her. Most of the time, she managed to fend for herself, shuffling between her daybed and the bathroom, eating from whatever pot of soup had been made for the week. But today she wanted Ana's attention. She patted the vacant space on the bed.

"I want to tell you something."

"Hmm," Ana said, absent-mindedly. She was thinking of the chores still needing to be done, the bills to be paid.

"I was going to tell you all this after the fire at your house, about what really happened," Margaret said.

Today Ana wasn't so sure she was up to one of Margaret's stories. They turned into lectures, sometimes, and she wasn't sure she was in the mood.

"What do you mean, what really happened?" she asked.

"The day the fire started. That day, it was hard to tell you anything."

"Okay, so what happened?" Ana said. There had been the fire in the forest. A freak accident. Lightning. Something. She was impatient, wanting to get to the kitchen to make breakfast.

"That pillowcase Emmy took everywhere with her," Margaret said. "All that stuff in it. Remember that?" There was a dull, rattling cough, and Margaret's face went a pale shade of gray. There were little flecks of saliva, spattering her lips and chin.

Ana wiped it off with a tissue. "You should rest," she said.

"It wasn't lightning that started that fire," Margaret said. "It was Emmy."

This was ridiculous, Ana thought. Margaret didn't know what she was saying.

"She must have swiped it, the cigarette lighter. From the counter. When you got your groceries. No one would ever have known, except I saw her do it. I got her out of there by the scruff of her neck, just before the fire took hold. She was shaking all over, holding that stupid pillowcase."

"That isn't possible," Ana said. But she began to feel an unnatural cold. She was no longer looking at Margaret, analyzing her.

"I went through everything," Margaret said, "and found the lighter. All she would say was that she was 'making a cookout.' She was scared as hell.

So it was true. Ana had bought those disposable lighters for Frank.

She might have left one on the counter. And it was true that Emmy had always been full of secrets. She remembered the slump of Emmy's shoulders that day, the tense arms that had refused to give up the pillowcase, the sooty look of those thin summer clothes. The way Emmy had buried her face in her shoulder, hiding. The belief took hold. "Why didn't you tell me?" she said.

"I couldn't. I don't know."

"Emmy lied? She let me believe she was safe with you?"

"You were lying to *her*, Ana. About other things," Margaret said.

Ana wanted to take Margaret and shake her. But she also wanted to throw her arms around her and hug her, to say thank you, to beg forgiveness, to wring what might be left of the life from her, so she could save it for her, give it back to her to use, so she could go back to her animals and land, to live. She was angry and grateful, all at once. She let tears slip down her cheeks without wiping them away.

"You said you believed in honesty." Margaret's face took on some color now, a redness spreading on the pale cheekbones. "You say that, but you do nothing but lie to yourself." She took big gulps of air to keep up with the effort of speaking. "You think I didn't know about that man you love? I know how that feels. I know. I love a man I can't ever hold again. I know. I love a child I can't ever hold again. You love a man and you're too chickenshit to do anything about it."

Ana couldn't deny it, but wanted to explain. "He doesn't want me any more," she said.

"If you've got a heart you'd better get out there and find out a way to get him back, or you're going to end up doing like I've done all these years. Always missing what I lost, never getting back to really living."

"How did you know?" Ana asked. There was no point in denying it.

"Like I told you before," Margaret said, "I know everything. I watch. I see things."

When did you figure it out?"

"When I met him at the hospital," Margaret said. "He said he recognized my name, said you had talked about me. He asked how you were. He seemed to me like a good man. I asked enough questions and got enough answers to know I was right about that. Besides, he had these moon-eyes when he talked about you. And don't think I didn't see that same look in your eyes whenever you used to leave Emmy with me."

Ana had never stopped thinking of Michael, had tried to gather her courage to see him again. But she had hesitated, thinking she should leave him alone, remembering her failures, his anger. She had decided, reluctantly, to get on with her life. Now she knew she wasn't going to ignore this curse, or blessing, or whatever it was Margaret was doing to her. It had been long enough. She had waited long enough, too long. It was time to get back to living.

"You're right," Ana said. "I am a chickenshit. And I'm going to do something about it."

Margaret smiled, a broad grin, a smile like Ana had not seen on her face in a long time.

◊ ◊ ◊

In November Ana went to the hospital, dressed to meet Michael, hoping he would be working. She had been afraid to call ahead, afraid of what he would say, of what he would do. She smoothed the skirt of the blue dress she'd worn at the China Dragon, wanting him to remember. Maybe then he could forgive her for what she'd done. After the information desk, there was one more turn in the hallway, and she would see him. She stopped walking halfway there, her heart pounding. There was a stairwell on the left, and on the right, a small balcony with a metal railing, overlooking an interior courtyard. She stepped onto the balcony, waiting, stopping to compose herself.

A skylight and side windows lit the courtyard dimly. Below, on the ground floor, a surgeon spoke gently to the family of an ICU patient. The sound of his words was faint, but Ana could just make them out: "Hairline fracture, on his spine, near the neck." It must have been the mother sobbing, and her answer. "He's only seventeen. He started walking when he was just over a year old."

Ana leaned into the railing, arms straight and tense, straining to hear the rest. But there were only sporadic, dismembered words.

"Paralyzed...three months...therapy." Her gaze wandered to the windows ahead of her. She could see the nurses in the lighted rooms as they worked. Even if she saw Michael, would she know what to say to him? She didn't know. She felt ashamed, uneasy, yet driven by her will to find him, to talk to him one more time.

A woman stepped into view, framed in fluorescent light, taking a chart from someone, another nurse, a man. Michael. She could see him bend down to pick up a tray, stand to adjust tubes and machines. It brought such a rush of longing as she watched him. She wanted to go straight in, to take his hand, to tell him she had never stopped loving him. She tried to smooth her hair back, clipped in a silver barrette, but it refused to be tamed, the wild curls escaping.

She opened the door and started down the hall. The nurse at the station said she should wait in the lounge. She sat on a narrow sofa facing a row of half-empty lockers, their doors ajar. She stared at them, remembering the first time they'd really talked, the smell of the tea he'd given her-cardamom and honey, the egg-shaped cup. The way he said he would teach her. She had forgotten, somehow, his promise.

"Ana," he said, suddenly standing beside her. She turned to meet his eyes. His face was tense, controlled.

"They put you in Pediatrics," she said. "You always said someday you'd burn out on the Psych Ward." She tried to make herself sound casual, as if her heart was not trying to pound its way out of her, beat by beat.

"A month ago," he said.

She let her eyes slip away from his, down to her hands that sat in her lap, upturned, surrendered. She spoke again, tentatively. She knew his eyes were still on her, unfaltering.

"I left Frank," she said. "I didn't think I ever could, but I did."

"Good," he said, but he didn't say more. She felt him waiting for her to go on, to say something that could explain how much power Frank had wielded, how she had been incapable of fighting it. She had to make him understand how she could have cheated him, and herself. How sorry she was.

"I never meant to do things the way I did," she said. "I don't even have a right to talk to you." She wondered if it had been a mistake to come here. She gathered the courage to go on.

"Michael, can you forgive-?"

"I don't know," he said.

Ana thought that his eyes looked through her, failed to see what she was trying to tell him. "I don't blame you if you hate me," she said.

He looked away then, back to the room where his patient was. "I don't know what to think any more. I'm not the same as I was before," he said.

"I'm not the same either," she answered. She hoped he would believe her, but he seemed determined to turn her away.

"Just say there's a chance," she said. She was suddenly aware of her hands, of how empty and useless they felt. She crossed her arms across her stomach, held herself in.

"I've got to get back to work."

"Can I see you again?"

"If you want."

It wasn't an invitation. It was only the result of the choices she'd made. She watched him leave, and he didn't look back. She left dejected, the hospital door swinging behind her. She lay awake all night, remembering every detail of their meeting, trying to accept the fact that it was, in fact, the only kind of meeting she had ever expected. But she couldn't stifle the memory of it, or resolve to leave behind all hope. In the morning, she went to the corner of the apartment where she'd set up the pottery wheel. It was a mess. She cleaned it out, rinsing tools and jars, scrubbing the table, sweeping the floor. It took a good hour to get the job done.

She took the soft, brown clay from its wrapping, drawing in the cool, earthy scent. She added scraps from a bucket, from her failures, the misshapen, stillborn pots, all the crooked jars and sagging bowls. She broke the clay down, losing herself in the gentle noise of it, the wet sound sloughing against her hands, palm to palm, massaging it like a fat, healthy baby. When she pushed against it her very body seemed to be the clay, yielding, ready to be shaped. She had finally learned how far it could be pulled and stretched before it collapsed in on itself, had learned when to be tender, slipping her fingers delicately around a fragile rim, persuading it. She had learned when to stop, allowing the work to harden, and most of the time, when to rest her hands.

Today, despite the thoughts of what had happened the day before, her hands were steady and sure, and she knew what the result of every movement would be. The clay was ready, the motor of the wheel humming against the silence. There was a moment's hesitation before she used the strength of her arms to slap the clay to the center of the stone, a moment of doubt, despite the weeks of practice. But when she let go and trusted, when she let her body speak for her, the doubt slipped away. She opened the clay, and the pot was born.

As it turned, her hands moved with it, fingertips meeting around the circle of the base, pulling the walls out and up, opening it to what it was to become. She felt sure of it, felt the give and take of the clay as she moved it, and when the pot took its final shape, she thought she could see something of a new beginning in it, something whole and sacred.

She slipped a knife under the base, releasing it from the stone. Before she put her tools away, she took one last glance at the pot. It was beautiful, fat and earthy, a glittering, silvery-brown. It had a broad base, even and solid, sloped upward to a sweet-sloped rim, like a mouth opening to song. She couldn't help but feel proud of it. And it made her smile, made her sure of her resolve. She was going to see Michael again.

19

*I*n December the doctors started Margaret on oxygen, which she agreed to use, and gave her a wheel chair, which she refused to sit in. Ana found her half naked late one night, gripping the kitchen sink, trying to get to the bathroom on her own. The room was a mess, urine-stained sheets, panties in a plastic bucket. The oxygen must have been off for a while because Margaret seemed confused. She'd gotten creative with the oversized t-shirt she was wearing. It was scrunched on her upper arms, the rest of it tugged all the way over her head, the neckhole gaping across her upper back like a straightjacket.

"You're a brat," Ana said. She gripped the handles of the wheel chair, till now tucked away in a corner of the dining room, and rolled it to Margaret, giving her a look. Margaret still gripped the sink, but weak, unsteady. "I'm just bringing this in case you want to sit down and rest a little." Margaret nodded and slumped into the chair, grimacing.

Ana wasn't about to rub it in, this small battle won. There was no joy in it, just relief that there might be less risk of Margaret breaking a leg as she dragged herself to the bathroom. "We might want to change that shirt," she said.

"I'm sorry." Margaret looked morose, ashamed.

"It's okay," Ana said. She wheeled her to the bathroom, helped her to the toilet, then began to wash the bed, the floor.

"You're pretty stinky," Ana said.

Margaret smiled, a little proudly. "Very bad?"

"Yeah."

"Like the cats?"

"Worse." Ana smiled then too. "Will you let us give you a bath?"

"Okay," Margaret said. "Just this once. Not between the toes, though."

"Ticklish?" Ana reached for her feet.

"Don't even think about it," Margaret said. She allowed the sponge bath, though. Emmy carried towels and washcloths, then stood back and stared wide-eyed at Margaret's long, broad body exposed and helpless, while Ana washed her, piece by piece. Emmy coughed a little and covered her mouth and nose.

Ana glanced at her. It must be tough for Emmy, she thought. It was hard enough for Ana to do this herself, to deal with the shock of learning how to nurse with no warning, no training, no choice but to do what must be done.

"You okay?"

Emmy nodded, still holding her hand up, and blinked hard, twice.

"Why don't you go watch TV for a while? Or that video you like?"

Emmy shook her head, dropped her hand, lifted her chin. "No," she said, looking not at Ana when she answered, but at Margaret, their eyes locked in what looked like a silent promise. "No. I want to help." She took a clean washcloth, dipped it in soapy water, squeezed it out. She was the one to wash Margaret's feet, never once touching the toes, concentrating on the sole, avoiding the instep, in case that was ticklish too. Then she blotted each foot with a towel, patting gently.

Ana was solemn. She hadn't been prepared for this-for the stench of disease, the coldness of waiting for death. But it was a relief to have Margaret cleaned up at last, to have her cooperate, for once. She stayed up with her late that night, and Emmy stayed too, curled up at the foot of Margaret's bed.

"Get the cremation done at that place on Garcia Street," Margaret said. "I don't want you spending too much. Direct Funeral Services. Cut-rate price. Nothing fancy."

"There's plenty of time to think about that," Ana said. She was thinking about it, though. Wondering when she should call them, what she would have to do.

"Don't be so sure," Margaret said. Her eyes were a muddy color, weary.

"I can stay with you tomorrow," Emmy said. "Since Momma has to work again."

"I can take off," Ana said.

"No," Margaret said. "You'll lose your job."

"The lady next door could come over," Emmy said. "She's nice. She left us a note when we made her that cake for helping last time."

"What note?" Margaret asked. "Read it to me."

Emmy scrambled up, rummaged through the papers on the kitchen table, bills, prescriptions, Margaret's overdue taxes. She found a wrinkled note on lined yellow paper and climbed back up to the bed.

"Dear Ana," she read. "Thank you for the cake. It's an honor to help such a nice family. The cake was dee-dee- "

"Delicious? Ana said.

"Yeah-Delicious," Emmy read. "Thanks again. P.S. Any time you need my help, just call me. Sin-sin-"

"Sincerely?" Ana said.

"Yeah," said Emmy. "Sincerely, Donetta."

Ana was flooded with gratitude, for the neighbor's help, for the kind words. She had found little reason, until this moment, to think about cheerful things, no matter how silly and small. She looked at Margaret's face, deep in its pillow, the expectant look. Not hopeless as Ana would have thought. She seemed at peace, the eyelids heavy, dropping. And that, somehow, was what set Ana free to cry as she hadn't before. She let go of the need to be strong.

"I feel stupid," she said. "Helpless."

Margaret nodded, almost smiling. "Me too."

"What will I do without you?" Ana said. The tears rolled down her face and onto the front of her pajama shirt, and she made no effort to stop them or wipe them away.

Margaret lifted a frail hand and stroked Ana's head, the fingers light, like the bones of a bird. "Do what's good for you and Emmy, and you'll be okay," she said.

Emmy wrapped her arms around Margaret's legs, as if to keep her from flying away. Outside the kitchen window, a full moon shone through the darkness, cold and bright, lighting Margaret's face.

Early in the morning, Ana sat on Emmy's bed and gently shook her shoulder to wake her.

"Go away," Emmy yawned, pulling her blanket over her head.

Ana pulled it back down. "Wake up," she said.

The blanket went up again.

"I'm going to teach you to make pots," Ana said.

"You're always too busy," the voice under the blanket said.

"I know. I'm sorry."

"When?" Emmy asked, revealing one eye.

"Whenever you want," Ana said. "I'll let you sleep, now. I just wanted to tell you that."

Emmy yawned, rubbed her eyes with her fists.

"Emmy?" Ana felt funny, like laughing and crying, all at the same time. "I love you, baby."

Ana made good on her promise. She taught Emmy as she worked, helping her with odd, leaky teapots, doll's cups and saucers, and more than once, ashtrays for Frank. In whatever room they were in, Emmy's lopsided pottery was displayed on a table or shelf. It was a small and tender thing between them, and Ana was grateful for it.

Two weeks before Christmas Margaret stopped breathing, and died. Only then did Ana realize how unprepared she was for this. Margaret had refused to leave a list of contacts, saying whoever was left of her family should not have to suffer because of her any longer. Ana had meant to write the things she knew of Margaret's life, but she had procrastinated. Now, it seemed impossible, but she had to write something. Only she and Emmy were left to remember her.

Margaret's body waited for its transport to the funeral home, the white deerskin boots on her feet, just as she'd asked. The cut glass beads had been sewn to them in exquisite design, turquoise, red, and black. Ana pulled a woolen blanket around her, tucked a basket into the folds, one with a star-flower woven of yellow and green yucca, the rim finished in fine, even stitches. At least she had made the final arrangements as Margaret had directed. There was nothing to do now but wait. She took a pen, felt it solid in her hand, one of those big metal ball-points with a rubber grip. She began to write.

Margaret.

1) A good wife, mother, friend.

2) Mescalero Apache, a black-eyed beauty.

3) Raised on a reservation in a two-room house. Remembered hunger.

4) A basket-maker, an artist. Loved animals.

It seemed no more was necessary, nothing more to be done. Ana stopped writing and surrendered to waiting. When they came to take Margaret away she realized the house would be clean again, quiet. But there would still be, like now, the chattering of the small blue parakeet, an occasional whistle and ruffle of feathers, the sound of Emmy shuffling about in her slippers, helping her take down the daybed, sweeping the floors, washing the dishes piled in the sink. There would be peace of a sort, but one that would be incomplete. There would still be things to attend to, things to finish.

20

The funeral home called to say Margaret's ashes were ready. Ana drove to get them in a drifted snow that had turned the asphalt to a mirrored sheen. She left the brown adobe building carrying a small, heavy package, feeling the snowflakes on her face, wet, silent. The drive to La Cueva seemed shorter than usual, the trek past the village with its sleepy adobes, its hand-painted signs, cheap motels and junk car lots. There was the mud-brown church with its blue Madonna, the weathered crosses, the river.

When she got to the road she parked where the gate used to be, pulled on her boots, and hiked up to the ridge, carrying the package. At the base of the ponderosa, she knelt to open it, lifted the urn from the wrapping, and opened it. She cupped a handful of Margaret's ashes and lifted spooned palms, again and again, tossing the ashes to the east, turning them loose. They flew in silvery clouds, settling to dust where the sun had come out to warm the ground. She could see Margaret in the buckskin dress rubbed with pollen shining yellow, could hear the sound of the tin jingles, like little bells. She saw her long black hair streaming behind her, the lift of her quick-stepping feet. She could hear Margaret's prayer for strength, long life, for happiness.

She stooped to scrape up some clay and marveled at the mica that glittered there. She had hated the caliche of the road, but now she understood. The earth was precious, the stuff of life. What had once been rock and mountain had been rained on, beaten down, filtered through sand and stone. It was pure, powerful, ready to be shaped into something new.

At Margaret's place, she checked on the animals, wondering how she would deal with them from here on out. Margaret had said they could go to the Humane Society, but Ana said no, she would keep driving out and taking care of them until she could find homes for them. She had made no real progress, so she'd lied a little, telling Margaret that one veterinarian knew of a family that would take in both cats, that a friend of her mother's would adopt the dogs. She lied even more about the chickens, saying those were slated for a free-range farm in Magdalena, one that only dealt in organic eggs. The truth was that she didn't have a clue what she was going to do, that she hadn't had time to do more than keep the animals fed and watered.

She made the trek home, and by the time she arrived, she had decided.

"I need help," she said into the telephone, having dialed, having found Michael on the line, as she'd hoped.

Now there was only silence on the line.

"You said I could call," she added, still hoping, waiting.

"Okay," he said, one of those long *okays* that had a question mark at the end, that didn't really mean "Okay" but "What?" and "Explain."

"My friend Margaret, the one you talked to in the hospital," she started. "She died."

"I'm sorry," he said, and then was quiet again.

"You always said you liked animals," she said, and then blushed, though no one was there to see her, because it sounded idiotic. He would have no way of knowing what she was getting at.

"I do," he said. But that didn't sound like *I do*, either. It sounded like: *I do, but what does that have to do with Margaret and why are you calling me?*

Ana swallowed hard and tried to think of how to say what she'd called to say. She couldn't think of a way to soften it or to make it sound like it was a sensible request, which she knew it wasn't. But she wanted to see Michael and she wanted to take care of the animals and she had no idea how she was going to do either one unless she got busy and did something radical like throw herself on his mercy and ask him for help. So she did, in one long breath of words.

"I know this is out of the blue and you don't owe me a thing but I don't know what else to do because Margaret had animals and they're homeless now and I can't take them in my apartment and I was wondering if you'd take some or all of them or if you could maybe keep them at your house until I can find homes for them, and I'm sorry to ask, but that's what I need."

"Ah," he started.

"Please don't say no," she said. "Just let me come out there and get you and take you up to her place and once you see them I know you'll like them, they're really nice animals, two dogs, two cats, three chickens-"

"Okay, okay," he said.

Ana's knees buckled in relief, her hand holding the receiver so tight her palm ached. "Okay," she said. "Thank you so much."

"Don't make a lot out of it," he said. He sounded serious, telling her not to get her hopes up. But still, he'd said yes.

"Can we come up now?"

"I'll be here," he said.

Ana drove herself and Emmy to his house in the Wagon, searching until she saw his house and the Cottonwoods, dark and wet with snow. She parked, left Emmy waiting, knocked on the front door.

He opened it, then looked over her head to where Emmy squirmed in the back seat, her freckled nose pressed into the window.

"So that's Emmy," he said. He got the keys to his house, put on a coat, and followed her. He ran his hand along the Wagon's fenders. "More rust than last time I saw it," he said.

"I know," she said. "I ought to put it out of its misery, but I feel sorry for it."

"Yeah," he said. "I know what you mean." He opened the passenger door and got in.

"Are you the man who's a nurse?" Emmy asked, yanking on her seat belt, pulling it loose so she could get a better look at him.

He twisted his body toward the back seat, so he could see her too. He held out his hand to her, and she put her small hand in his and shook it.

"That's me," he said. "Michael Woods." And you're the famous Emmy?"

"Yup," she said.

"Why do you have a ponytail?" Emmy asked.

Ana could see her in the rear view mirror, staring at his head. She turned the key in the ignition, backed out of the driveway. She was impulsive, this child of hers. But in a good way. She was afraid of nothing, no one.

"I don't always have a ponytail," Michael answered. He loosed the tie and his hair fell long and wild, just as Ana remembered it.

Emmy snorted. "You've got a lot of hair!"

He turned around again, reaching to tug her hair, teasing her. "And you've got nice braids," he said.

"Yup," Emmy said. She grinned, a long gap where her front teeth used to be, and Ana almost laughed.

"We have a sad thing to do," Emmy said.

"I heard." Michael looked at Ana. "Pick up some animals," he said.

"Margaret's animals," Emmy said.

"Two dogs, two cats," he said.

"And chickens," Ana said.

"Chickens," he said, somber, sounding worried. He rubbed his chin, then scratched the back of his neck.

"Big, fat ones!" Emmy said. "And they're mean!"

When they got to Henry's concrete-block house they ground through the mud, past the sound of the rottweilers' barking, the faded green Chevy. The hill seemed shorter than before, but the mud pit was on the other side, as always. It was a blessing that it hadn't rained again, Ana thought. She pushed through a watery place where the culvert should have been, but the rest was plain, rutted earth. The Wagon still had to lumber up, the balding tires pulling, straining against the road.

On the last long stretch, the house-now Frank's house-came into view. She could see it through the trees, the curve of its roof tiles solid, impermeable. He had finished the house completely. The windows were double-hung, wood-framed, the glass shining like dark, clean water. She looked for the truck and saw it there, the Winchester in the rear window. She could picture Frank in the living room, alone, his feet kicked up on the footrest of the La-Z-Boy, a cigar tucked into the side of his lips, gray smoke curling upward. The thought of it filled her lungs, her nostrils. Thick. Stifling. She was glad the window was rolled down, that the cold winter air was slapping her face, reminding her that there was no smoke here.

It came to her now, she didn't feel his watching. She knew now what she never knew before. He was a small man, really. He hadn't bothered her all these months since the divorce. Just took Emmy on weekends, took care of her, brought her back when it was time. It seemed a long time ago that she'd been so afraid of him. It seemed crazy now, to think of it, now that he had let her go, that she'd never believed he would.

At Margaret's place she realized she hadn't thought out how to carry the chickens. But they found an oversized cardboard box, one side ready to buckle, the other bulging. Margaret had clearly used it before. On it was her printing, straight up and down in thick black Magic Marker-lines slashed through a whole history of labels: "Winter Clothes," "Pressure Cooker," "Shoes." They folded the lid to keep the hens inside, then loaded the cats into crates they found in Margaret's bedroom. One was the cat with a pendulous belly, the other one white with a plumed tail, like a royal eunuch.

In the motorhome, they wrapped baskets in tissue, stacked plates and cups, scrubbed the floors of the kitchenette. The clothes remaining were folded, stacked in the back of the Wagon with bead boxes, bags of feathers, tin-snips, willow. There was a box of envelopes, one that held the deed to Margaret's place, signed over to Ana. "You take it or I'm never speaking to you again," Margaret had said when Ana protested. It hadn't felt right. Ana had begged her to try to find her uncle or some kind of family, but to no avail. "You sell it," Margaret insisted. "Get a place of your own. Or get a place with that Nurse-Man, whenever you two decide to get together. You're my family," she'd said. "You take it." Ana had finally agreed, when she'd said that. It was true. Margaret was sister, aunt, mother, friend. She smiled a little, to think of it, while she loaded up bags of chicken mash, buckets of dog chow, the old green Coleman lanterns.

The cats and dogs were put in the Wagon last. While Ana started the engine, Emmy struggled to keep the dogs still, gripping their scarred leather leashes, holding tight. But she managed to stretch the seatbelt loose, to lean all the way to the front seat, resting her chin there, staring at Michael again.

"Gee-eesh," she said. "Bad dogs."

Michael leaned back, watching her, and tried not to laugh.

Printed in the United States
102920LV00004B/49-66/A

9 780865 345881